S0-CDO-780

"WHAT DO YOU THINK I'M DOING HERE?"

"Well, you had business in L.A. and—"

"And I just happened to work you into my schedule?" Greg smiled gently.

Renee shrugged and bit her lower lip. "Something like that."

He cupped her chin in his palm and tilted her head so that her eyes met his. "Do you think I could make love to you in Hawaii and that would be the end of it?"

Renee swallowed deeply, the pounding of her heart increasing. She didn't want to hear him say any of this. It was wrong. For both of them.

"My God, Renee," he said, his voice thick with emotion. "I'm in love with you."

Suddenly she wanted to cry. Oh, Lord, how in the world was she going to handle this now? "Greg, I—I don't know what to say."

"You don't have to say anything. Just tell me what the guy in those photographs means to you. Because if there's something important going on here, I want to know. Now."

AFTER THE LOVING

Samantha Scott

A CANDLELIGHT ECSTASY ROMANCE ®

Published by
Dell Publishing Co., Inc.
1 Dag Hammarskjold Plaza
New York, New York 10017

Copyright © 1984 by Samantha Scott

All rights reserved. No part of this book may be reproduced or transmitted in any form or by any means, electronic or mechanical, including photocopying, recording or by any information storage and retrieval system, without the written permission of the Publisher, except where permitted by law.

Dell ® TM 681510, Dell Publishing Co., Inc.

Candlelight Ecstasy Romance®, 1,203,540, is a registered trademark of Dell Publishing Co., Inc., New York, New York.

ISBN: 0-440-10050-X

Printed in the United States of America
First printing—January 1984

To Our Readers:

We have been delighted with your enthusiastic response to Candlelight Ecstasy Romances®, and we thank you for the interest you have shown in this exciting series.

In the upcoming months we will continue to present the distinctive, sensuous love stories you have come to expect only from Ecstasy. We look forward to bringing you many more books from your favorite authors and also the very finest work from new authors of contemporary romantic fiction.

As always, we are striving to present the unique, absorbing love stories that you enjoy most—books that are more than ordinary romance.

Your suggestions and comments are always welcome. Please write to us at the address below.

Sincerely,

The Editors
Candlelight Romances
1 Dag Hammarskjold Plaza
New York, New York 10017

CHAPTER ONE

Renee sat up in sudden agitation, grimacing as she spat yet another grain of sand from her teeth. "Yuk!" she exclaimed under her breath. Glancing up from beneath the wide rim of her sunhat, she smirked at the retreating pair of legs that had just kicked up a spray of sand into her face. This scene was getting old really fast, she thought heatedly, leaning back onto her elbows and extending her legs out in front of her once more.

Beneath the speckled, wide-framed Anne Klein lenses her dark brown gaze perused the surrounding Waikiki beach. Incredible, she thought for the countless time. A wall-to-wall sea of undulating bodies, either reclining or walking or running. Certainly the most well-greased nut-brown sea of human flesh she had ever laid eyes upon. And all those bodies were here for the same reason—a wonderful sun-filled few days or weeks of fun and relaxation. None of which, unfortunately, Renee Michaelson happened to be enjoying at the moment.

Such was the case, in fact, for almost the entire time she'd been here. With an expression filled with irony she surveyed the lean curves of her bikini-clad figure, the culmination of weeks—no months—of situps and sidebends and three-mile jogs done religiously. Just thinking about all that effort could make her tired. She could honestly say she was at her absolute fittest and if she said so herself, her most gorgeous. But what good was it doing her? Certainly her physical attributes hadn't impressed Louis. Not enough to keep him home this summer.

The mere thought of that depressing subject evoked a disgusted inward groan from Renee. Flopping onto her stomach, she crossed her arms and cradled her head between them. She closed her eyes, hoping to drift off while her back took its turn roasting. But the ugly thought had already invaded and there was no getting rid of it this time.

One thing she'd learned on this incredibly boring vacation that was for sure—one could not run from one's problems and troubles. Indeed, they had followed right along, and Renee had long since begun to wonder if she'd merely wasted her time and money coming all this way with Marcy.

Ironically, she'd latched onto the idea the second Marcy had suggested it. Louis had been gone only four days and already she'd been miserable, working like a madwoman at the hospital and moping around the house as though inflicted with some dread disease.

Damn it! Renee cursed inwardly. Why did she

have to be so upset over their separation? Especially when it was achingly apparent that Louis wouldn't be bothered in the least. Oh, no, not good old independent-minded Louis. She should have known he would pull something like this one day. But she'd let her hopes grow that perhaps he'd adjusted to a one-on-one relationship. After all, they'd been seeing each other exclusively for almost a year.

A green-eyed monster insidiously edged its way into the foreground of her thoughts, providing technicolor images of exactly what she suspected he was up to at this very moment. The mere thought of him doling out all that charm, wit, that animal magnetism, made her want to chew nails. How could he do this to her! Make her feel so damn miserable while he was out cavorting with who knows who all over Zurich or wherever else he was playing.

Angrily, Renee pushed herself up on her elbows, just in time to catch another mouthful of sand as someone walked by.

"Forget it!" she exclaimed in a voice loud enough to be heard, then pushed back, sitting on her heels as she brushed the grains of sand off her face and arms. This certainly wasn't getting her anywhere, lying on the beach feeling absolutely miserable. She might be foolish about getting so depressed and down in the mouth about Louis, but one thing she wasn't—extravagant. She damned sure wasn't going to waste *all* her hard-earned money lying around feeling sorry for herself.

Just look at this place, Renee. All this beauty, all this luxury. She was suddenly overwhelmed by an urge to forget her frustrations, to jump in and enjoy whatever she could of it. Even if that meant kicking a little sand in someone else's eyes. Rolling up her towel, she placed it under her arm, then slipped into her thongs. She pushed the sunglasses back up the bridge of her nose, pulled her hat down low over her forehead, and set off.

She walked aimlessly for a while, enjoying the tickle of foaming surf bubbling up over her feet. Her gaze wandered out over the water, watching surfers paddling outward or crouched down low on their boards, awaiting the perfect wave to ride out back to the shore. The walk was refreshing but most of all relaxing. For once Renee's thoughts were successfully diverted from the track they'd remained glued to the past few weeks.

She looked behind to gauge how far she'd walked and was astounded to see it had been several hundred yards. She glanced at her watch and suddenly remembered that she was supposed to meet Marcy for lunch at the hotel at one o'clock. That was thirty minutes from now. Perfect. It would give her something to do and, besides, she was beginning to feel faintly hungry by now.

She turned back, then walked a few paces before stopping dead in her tracks. Her gaze riveted on a figure emerging from the water some twenty yards offshore. Renee watched in fascination as a man rose slowly, like some mythical sea god, from the waves rushing up behind and around him. With a toss of his head a shock of dark hair that lay against his forehead was flung backward, exposing a square, deeply bronzed forehead. Her gaze swept downward across evenly tanned, beautifully carved features—she could only wonder at the color of his eyes from this distance—then down the strong, muscular column of his neck.

He was tall; she could tell that even before he completely emerged from the water. He raised both hands to wipe the water off his face and Renee was absolutely fascinated by the play of muscles along his arms and broad shoulders. A flat stomach complemented the trim waist and lean hips and as he emerged fully onto the beach Renee was awed by the perfectly toned body.

She swallowed unconsciously as she allowed her gaze to travel farther downward, focusing upon an incredible pair of thighs, long and lean yet almost bulging in their highly developed state. The man stood still for a moment at the edge of the water, and Renee felt a warm flushing sensation wash over her entire body. The small piece of cloth that constituted his swim suit was tauntingly revealing, and it was more than she could handle to focus her eyes on what she was doing. What *was* she doing?

To anyone observing her it was obvious that she was gaping. But it was impossible not to. The man was positively unbelievable. He moved onto the beach with the fluid grace of a stalking lion, unaffectedly displaying his body in all its masculine glory. He hadn't noticed her, wasn't looking at anything or anyone as he made his way along the edge of the beach away from her.

Suddenly Renee's feet were propelled into action and she began to walk, her steps quickening as she followed several yards behind him. Inexplicably, she was seized with the urge, the necessity, not to let this man get away. At least not until she knew where he was headed. Her breathing was coming in rapid, shallow spurts by the time she stopped, once more in the midst of a carpet of bodies in various reclining positions. She watched as he entered a roped-off area adjacent to one of the hotels.

Most of the beachfront hotels had such private enclosures, and Renee had wished on more than one occasion that she and Marcy had had the foresight to make reservations at one of them. Suddenly an image of how she must look just standing there flitted before her mind's eye—a leering, dirty old lady, getting her kicks scoping out a gorgeous hunk of male skin. Well, so what? What's sauce for the goose is definitely sauce for the gander.

She wiped a rivulet of perspiration from her cleavage with her forefinger, glancing around to find another empty spot to throw out her beach towel. Finding one, she positioned it so that Mr. Gorgeous was in her direct line of vision. She lay down and propped herself back on her elbows and threw her head back, allowing her face to absorb the burning rays of the sun. Unbidden, Louis's figure loomed before her reddened lids and she asked herself for what surely must have been the umpteenth time what he was probably doing right now.

Damn it! What was wrong with her? Why couldn't she just forget about him for at least one day? Was he wondering about her now, worried about what she was up to? You could bet your sweet tootsies he wasn't, she reflected with the usual irritation. Hell, if he'd been even half as concerned as she was, he'd have asked her to come with him. But he hadn't. And she was driving herself nuts hashing and rehashing a subject that didn't merit it anyway. He was there, fifteen-thousand miles away, and she was here . . . and there was nothing she could do about it.

She opened her eyes then and peered through the dark lenses of her sunglasses. As if by magnetism her gaze was pulled in the direction of the hotel-partitioned beach area. He was still there, half-sitting, half-reclining against a padded portable sand chair. He appeared to be sleeping; his eyes were closed, his arms resting on either side of his long, supple body, one leg flexed, the knee pointed upward.

Inhaling deeply, Renee turned onto her side, laying her head on her outstretched arm. Another spray of sand scattered across the backs of her legs as someone carelessly walked by behind her. She was oblivious to the incident this time, however, as her gaze remained fixed on the handsome man lying twenty yards away. He turned his head in her direction suddenly, and Renee was instantly afraid he'd noticed her staring at him. But that was crazy. There were too many people for him to even distinguish her among them, and, besides, her hat and sunglasses were protection enough.

He turned away slowly, but not before Renee glimpsed the expression on his tawny face. His well-chiseled features held an expression of total boredom. Strange, she mused. How could anyone that gorgeous be bored? Then he reached for a book which lay next to him and opened it to the middle. It was a big fat paperback, and she vaguely recognized the shiny foil and green cover. If it was what she thought it was . . . Hmmm, that was interesting.

Suddenly she flopped onto her back. What in the world was she doing? Talk about bored! How much time had she just wasted analyzing this complete stranger? A damned good-looking one at that but still it was . . .

She saw him out of the corner of her eye just then and crazily her heart began to trip erratically. He had gotten up and was walking directly toward her! God, surely he hadn't seen her staring. Then he stopped very near her, placed a fist on his hip, and shaded his eyes with the other hand. He turned his head slowly from right to left, and it was obvious then that he hadn't seen her at all. He appeared to be looking for someone, and he stood there that way for several minutes.

Renee was unnerved by his presence and wished he would go away. On the other hand she couldn't keep her eyes off him and, slowly, insidiously, an idea crept into her mind. What if the situation were altered a bit and she were Louis lying here, eyes trained on some beautiful female specimen mere inches away. What would he do in such a situation? Renee's eyelids narrowed a fraction as the uncomfortable answer came to her immediately. She had no concrete evidence of course, but the intuition was there, and she'd long ago come to trust that facet of her personality implicitly. She knew damn well what he'd do.

She sat up then and stretched out her legs in front of her, leaning back on her hands and arching her back just the tiniest bit. It was outright, shameless preening, and it wasn't long before his head turned once more in her direction. But if Renee had thought his eyes would suddenly become glued to her, she was embarrassingly disappointed. Instead, he appeared to be scanning the beach scene once again, and she wondered what could be so all-fired important that he was looking for.

He stuck his head out just a little, as if he saw something, then took a few steps. A couple of kids came running along, shrieking and shouting at one another, and suddenly one of them pushed the other hard, knocking him directly against the tall man's backside. The man absorbed the blow of the light young body easily but for a moment was thrown somewhat off-balance. He stepped sideways and turned suddenly as if to catch the youngster, in the process kicking up a hefty spray of sand, all of it right onto Renee.

She sat straight up, muttering a definitely unladylike expletive in a voice loud enough to carry a few feet. Disgustedly, she began to brush the hot grains off her legs and stomach.

"I'm very sorry. I didn't mean to be so clumsy. It was those silly . . ."

Renee looked up, her gaze locking instantly with a startling pair of drenching, grass-green eyes. Almost iridescent in their intensity, they were framed by thick black lashes and set within a dark, brawny visage.

She struggled inwardly for a moment, to regain her composure, then said, "It doesn't matter. In fact, I've gotten rather used to it." She motioned with her head. "It doesn't matter where you choose, there's another body a few centimeters away."

"Would you like to join me over there?" The stranger nodded in the direction of the roped-off hotel area. "It's the same sand, but I guarantee not so much of it will end up in your face."

Renee laughed and lifted her shoulders. "Sounds ideal. But I'm not a guest. They might . . ."

"No problem. You'll be my guest if anyone even cares enough to ask."

Renee stood and quickly gathered up her things. "And just in case anyone does, who should I say is my host?"

The rugged, tanned face opened up in a wide, toothsome grin. "Greg Daniels. And the guest's name?"

"Renee Michaelson."

"Nice to meet you, Renee. C'mon, follow me."

And she did, not believing she was actually doing so. *But why not?* a tiny inner voice demanded. Do you think *he'd* do any different? A flash of Louis's charming, ever-calculating features plastered itself across her brain and suddenly Renee was filled with a determination and sense of purpose she hadn't experienced in ages. This was definitely more like the old Renee Michaelson.

Within a few minutes she was stretched out comfortably on a padded lounger next to Greg Daniels, well protected from the nuisance of the public beach crowd.

"Why don't you take those off?" he asked. He was lying on his side, fully stretched out; he'd have made the perfect tanning lotion poster, Renee thought.

"Take what off?"

"Your sunglasses. They cover up half your face."

Renee laughed and reached up to pull them off. "Is

that better? Are you satisfied you didn't make a mistake by inviting a one-eyed ghoul to join you?"

Greg's green gaze studied her features for a moment, then traveled slowly down her body, openly absorbing every inch of her. "Oh, yes," he said in a low, husky tone. "I'm pretty satisfied."

Renee tingled inwardly from the remark, and she squirmed unconsciously. She put the sunglasses back on and said, "Well, I can't leave them off. My contacts can't take the brightness."

He raised his brows questioningly. "So those beautiful dark brown eyes aren't really yours, are they?"

"Of course they're mine. What's that supposed to mean?"

"Most people that I know with contact lenses wear tinted ones."

"And so do I. But they're not brown. They're blue."

"Come on. Blue contacts with brown eyes. That's ridiculous."

Renee jolted upright and placed one hand on her hip, cocking her head to the side. "Hey, are you calling me a liar?"

Greg shrugged nonchalantly. "You said it, not me."

Renee frowned in mock offense, then said, "I've only just met you. You don't know a thing about me. And you have the audacity to call me a liar?"

The grass-green eyes sparkled challengingly. "True enough. I don't know you. But something can be done about that."

"Like what?"

"Have supper with me tonight." His eyes traveled to her left hand, which lay on the mat in front of her. "Unless . . . you're not available."

Renee grinned and flexed her hand; she'd caught his appraising look. "Sure, I'm available." *Did you hear that, Louis Mandol?*

Greg grinned his satisfaction. "Good. Where are you staying, Renee Michaelson?"

She told him and from then on the conversation between them flowed naturally, as if they'd known each other for far longer than a mere few minutes. The incredible briefness of his swim trunks—one could easily consider that a misnomer—was distracting, to say the least, and Renee found herself having to make a concerted effort to keep her eyes from wandering down the broad expanse of his deeply bronzed chest and the endless, powerfully developed legs. But he was easy to talk to and she found their bantering quite refreshing and enjoyable.

Eyeing the fat paperback that lay beside him, she asked, "Are you a big fan of Leslie Freemont's?"

Greg picked up the book and absently thumbed the edges. "Not really. I like his style and some of the 'messages' he throws in, but other than that . . . I don't read everything he writes. You?"

"Yeah, I really like him," Renee said, immediately launching the conversation in another direction.

It was a full two hours before either of them noticed the time, but it had nothing to do with running out of things to say. When was the last time she and Louis had indulged in such a long-winded discussion of virtually every noteworthy modern novelist? Last time? Hell, they *never* had. Louis hated novels, had absolutely no time for any reading that wasn't directly related to his work.

"Are you hungry?" Greg asked, standing and extending a hand to help Renee up.

"Starved. I forgot all about lunch."

Greg grinned. "Me too." Renee gathered up her things and stood looking up at him, her five-feet-six-inch frame fairly dwarfed by his imposing height. "How long do you take to get ready?"

Renee shrugged lightly. "Depends on where I'm going and what I'm supposed to wear."

"Well, what I had in mind is sort of dressy, you could say."

"Hmmm. Dressy takes at least an hour."

"Then why don't I meet you in the lobby of your hotel around six thirty?"

Renee smiled broadly. "Okay." She hesitated for a second, then added, "Uh, Greg?"

"Yes?"

"Oh, nothing . . . I'll see you then."

"All right."

She watched him walk off toward the lobby of his hotel then turned to walk back the way she'd come. She'd wanted to tell him thank you. But that would have sounded silly.

But she was grateful to him, very much so. For the first time in much too long a while she'd actually gotten her mind off Louis and what he was doing without her. Greg Daniels, she thought smugly, might be just exactly what the doctor ordered.

CHAPTER TWO

"You're kidding." Marcy stared at Renee's image in the mirror, watching as Renee methodically went through every garment, both hers and Marcy's, hanging in the closet. Marcy's long narrow face was smudged completely brown, her soft hazel eyes staring out hugely from the facial mask. She had just applied it and as she reached up to finger it lightly to see how well it had set, she turned around, leaning back against the vanity.

"I can't believe what I'm hearing. Renee Michaelson actually went and got herself a date? Mmm-*mmm.* Will wonders never cease. What brought this on?"

"Oh, would you shut up," Renee said, holding out a lavender silk dress. "How do you think this would do?"

"Where are you going?"

"He said somewhere sort of dressy."

"Well, that ought to fill the bill." Marcy folded her arms over her chest and cocked her head to one side. "You're not gonna get very far with this evasive bit, Renee."

"What do you mean, evasive? I just told you I have a date with a very good-looking man tonight. What else is there to say?"

"Oh, maybe a little insight as to what made you finally break down and forget about the 'fabulous' Louis for a few minutes. I'm certain it wasn't anything I said. You never take my advice."

Renee brushed past her friend and lay the dress smoothly across her double bed. "You're really a pest, you know that, Lindstrom."

"Yeah, yeah, whoop-de-do." Marcy flopped down onto her bed, leaning back onto her elbows. "Now cut the crap, Michaelson. Did this have anything to do with the fact that you stood me up for lunch today?"

Renee reached up to check the electric rollers in her hair. They were cooled by now, and she began taking the pins out. "Oh, yeah. Sorry about that, but as a matter of fact it did. But there's no big deal to it, Marcy. I just happened to meet this guy—man I should say—and he invited me to join him on the beach. What can I say? He's good-looking and has a nice personality and—" She paused, then added, "Is just what the doctor ordered."

"Well, I agree with that, but"—Marcy frowned—"somehow I get the impression that means something else to you than it does to me."

"It just means that I've been getting a little bored around here, and I can't see wasting all my time and money doing absolutely nothing. I could have done that at home."

Marcy sat up and pointed out, "You've had plenty of opportunities to do something other than lounge around on the beach and—"

"And, I'm sorry, I just don't dig your exploring routine." Renee shrugged and walked into the dressing area and began replacing the rollers in their case.

"No, you'd rather stick around and feel sorry for yourself."

"Not anymore," Renee answered with a sing-song tone.

There was silence for a moment, then Renee began applying her makeup. She heard the bedsprings bounce a little as Marcy got off the bed, then joined her at the dressing table.

"I don't like the sound of that," Marcy said warily.

Without her contacts on Renee had to stick her face mere inches from the mirror to see what she was doing.

"Sound of what?" she asked in a mumbled tone, one eye shut as she precariously smudged eyeshadow across one eyelid.

"What are you trying to pull, Renee?"

"I'm not trying to pull anything. Goodness, Marcy, I'm just going out with a guy; don't make it into a federal case."

"Yeah, but I know you, and you're doing this for all the wrong reasons. You're just doing it to get back at Louis."

Renee finished with the eye she was working on and opened it to stare back at her friend. "Well, so what? It's no different than what he's probably doing right now."

Marcy rolled her eyes. "God, when are you ever gonna learn? *Sure* it's what he's doing right now. You've been convinced of that since the day he left." Her voice softened and rose at the same time. "Don't you see what you're doing, Renee? Just going out with one guy to get back at another isn't going to do anyone any good at all. What about *you?*"

Renee said nothing, merely began working on the other eye. She'd heard most of this, or some version of it, too many times already. What could she possibly say that she hadn't already? Marcy disapproved of her relationship with Louis, thought she could get someone far more loving and certainly more trustworthy. But Renee loved Louis, and to her, love was a serious matter, something that didn't simply vanish overnight, or within the course of a separation. There were problems, sure, but she could deal with them in her own way, and in her own time. If she chose to see someone else to perhaps even the score, well, it might seem ridiculous to Marcy, but it made all the sense in the world to her.

"Look, Marcy," she said in a tired-sounding voice. "I know you really mean all this, and I know how much you think I should start seeing someone else besides Louis for my own good. Well, that's what I'm doing. Okay?"

Marcy's mouth narrowed into a disbelieving smirk and she returned to the bedroom and flipped on the television. "Okay, I'll quit bugging you, but not okay you're right and I'm wrong. You'll see."

Renee made no reply and the television news filled

the ensuing silence. She glanced at her watch and saw that she had only fifteen minutes before she was to meet Greg in the lobby. Quickly she slipped into the lavender dress, stepped into pair of ankle-strapped heels, and brushed out her soft light-brown hair. Marcy returned to the bathroom to start her bath and was busy setting out her own clothes for a party she'd been invited to by friends who lived in Honolulu. By the time Renee was ready to leave, Marcy was already in the tub and there was only time for a quick good-bye and a "See ya later."

Bobby McGee's Original Restaurant wasn't exactly what Renee had imagined when Greg told her he was taking her somewhere "sort of dressy." There were plenty of people dressed to the nines, so to speak, but just as many in a far more casual mode of attire. Nevertheless, the place was interesting, noisy, with lots of thirties and forties tunes, and scads of cleverly costumed waiters and waitresses running around. Despite the reservations Greg had made, they had to wait fifteen minutes for a table, but as Renee quickly discovered, a far longer wait would have been well worth it. The food was absolutely delicious.

"You look starved," Greg commented with a grin as he sat watching her almost wolf down the mushroom and zucchini appetizer.

Renee covered her full mouth with her hand, embarrassed at what she must look like. Greg was merely sipping his bourbon and water, looking as cool and self-possessed as he had earlier this afternoon. Not a few female heads had turned as they entered the restaurant earlier. Greg was sportily attired in a pair of off-white chinos with a tan and white striped shirt and a navy blazer. His dark brown hair was much fuller than it had appeared this afternoon all wet and plastered to his head. But his eyes were exactly the same, the vibrant, grass-green color compelling in intensity, like two glinting jewels one could not resist staring into.

"I hardly had a thing to eat all day," Renee said somewhat defensively. Then, lifting one shoulder, she cast him a sheepish glance. "Sorry if I'm embarrassing you. I must look like a glutton."

Greg chuckled lightly and cast her an appraising look. "As a matter of fact, you do. But don't worry about it. I'm a helluva one myself at times."

Renee laughed outright as his disarming frankness and any vestige of remaining shyness disappeared instantly. The rest of the food they'd ordered was just as delicious, and after they'd finished, Renee sat back and placed a hand over her upper abdomen.

"Ohh, I don't think I can move. Why did you let me do that?"

"Do what?" Greg asked, sipping at his cup of coffee.

"Let me eat all that food. I'll never make it out of here."

"Sure you will. Besides, I was counting on sharing dessert with you."

Renee's eyes widened disbelievingly. "You've gotta be kidding. There's no way, believe me."

Greg feigned disappointment and snapped his fingers. "Shucks. I was counting on it." His face brightened then, and he leaned forward a bit. "Tell you what. How about a dance to make me feel better?"

The music from the adjacent disco section of the restaurant had been changing over the past hour and a half, progressing from thirties and forties sounds to hits from the fifties, and was now featuring songs from the early sixties, some of Renee's favorites. She smiled back at Greg.

"Sure. Might make me feel a little better to move around too."

The dance floor was crowded, but Greg managed to locate a minuscule spot for the both of them. The number switched to a slow one and as Greg's arms encircled her, Renee slid one of her own around his back and placed the other atop his shoulder. She kept her head back for a moment, then rested her chin just below his shoulder. Nice. Very nice.

She hadn't danced in such a long time, Renee reflected. Louis hated to dance; wild horses couldn't drag him onto a dance floor, let alone give her the chance to nestle up against him as she was doing now. With someone else. She really liked this feeling of gliding along, secure within the strong arms pulling her so close. If she closed her eyes, she could imagine that it *was* Louis holding her, dancing so smoothly and effortlessly with her through the crowded dance floor.

She drew in a deep breath and her eyes opened suddenly.

The warm, spicy scent that filled her nostrils was certainly not Louis. All Louis ever smelled like was Louis. He never had time for anything as "trite" as cologne. Hell, he hardly had time for her, come to think of it. The thought angered Renee freshly and she considered the fragrance Greg was wearing. It wasn't bad. Not bad at all.

Greg pulled away slightly just then and said, "Kind of hard to move in here, isn't it?"

Renee hadn't noticed at all. She lifted her shoulders in a noncommittal answer and Greg smiled down at her, then pulled her back to him. Renee gulped, aware of a crazy spasm in her stomach. Strange that she should feel something as *physical* as that. The idea of it was alarming. Good Lord, she hadn't felt *anything* for anyone since she and Louis had been together. The niggling suspicion crept up on her, as it had so often in the past few weeks, that the case might not be the same for Louis. Damn it, she wasn't supposed to be dwelling on thoughts like that. Not now at least.

The song ended soon and Greg found them a table along the perimeter of the dance floor. They had only just taken their seats when the loudspeakers began blaring out a hit rock number and it was clear any conversation would have to be done at a shout.

"Would you like to leave?" Greg practically yelled at her. Renee nodded that yes, she would.

A moment later they were standing in the balmy night air just outside the restaurant. "Do you want to take a cab back or would you care to walk?" They had taken a cab over, but the idea of a walk sounded particularly inviting to Renee who was just beginning to lose that uncomfortable fullness in her stomach.

"As a matter of fact, I'd like to walk."

As they strolled down the boulevard that led back

into the downtown area, Greg took Renee's hand in his. Silvery rays from a bright full moon glistened upon the midnight-blue expanse of ocean beyond, silhouetting the ancient banyon trees, sharpening the jagged angles of Diamond Head. What a perfect setting, Renee thought, pleasantly amazed at how comfortable she was in Greg's presence, especially considering that they'd only met hours earlier.

"How do you like living in Seattle, Greg?" She was referring to his reference earlier that it wasn't his hometown. He'd lived there for only the past couple of years.

"Actually, it's not too bad. As long as you invest heavily in raincoats and galoshes."

Renee laughed. "C'mon, the weather's not that bad, is it? I've heard it's really pretty."

"Oh, it is. But it does rain a lot."

"What is it exactly that you do in your job? I really didn't understand what you meant earlier."

Greg smiled that marvelously warm smile. "Well, it's really exactly what I told you. I'm in sales. Only my product is a little larger than the usual. I sell Seattle."

Renee laughed lightly. "Now what does that mean?"

Greg looked at her guilelessly. "Just what I said. I sell the city of Seattle as a convention locale for various national organizations. Doctors, lawyers, nurses, political groups, truckers . . . you name it. I'm employed by the city government."

"How in the world did you end up in such a position? It sounds really interesting."

Greg nodded. "Actually, it is. To answer your

question, it was a case of falling into the job so to speak. They certainly didn't come looking for me. Not all the way out in Norman, Oklahoma."

Renee looked at him in surprise. "Is that where you're from?"

"Yup," Greg drawled in a quite authentic-sounding southern accent. "Farm bred and raised. Jes an ole country boy."

Renee laughed at his apt imitation, suddenly picturing him in another, altogether different setting. Understandably, rural Oklahoma suddenly took on a rather intriguing appeal. How many more of these handsome "farm-boys" had it spawned? she wondered.

Shaking her head, she said, "Somehow I can't picture you milking cows, Greg Daniels."

"Oh, but I did." He held out his hands before her. "These here are the best set of yankers you'll ever lay your big brown eyes on, lady."

Again she laughed, thoroughly enjoying his refreshing, unpretentious attitude about himself. He wasn't faking it, somehow she knew that for certain. He probably *had* milked quite a few of those bovine creatures, the thought of which made him seem even more real, more down-to-earth than his disarming good looks would lead one to believe. What a neat person he was, the thought popped through her head.

"So how did you manage to pull yourself away from the farm and end up in Seattle, Washington?"

"My mother's family was from there. Her brother, who's been involved in the city government for a long time, recommended me for the position—and the position to me. I'd been involved in marketing and sales ever since I graduated."

"Ah ha," Renee said, her eyes sparkling teasingly. "So the farm boy did manage to make it in the big city a few times, eh?"

"Yup. Sure did."

"Well, I must say, Mr. Daniels, you've had quite an interesting background. I suppose you have to travel a lot."

"Mmmhmm. Quite a lot as a matter of fact." Greg hesitated then asked, "So what about you? How did you end up in personnel?"

"Hard work, of course. Well," she smiled ruefully, "maybe a little luck too. The position opened up just when I happened to be perfectly ripe for it."

Greg cast her a speculative glance. "That doesn't tell me very much."

Renee shrugged. "Well, what do you want to know? Personnel isn't really all that interesting."

"Well . . . for starters you could tell me where you're from. Who your parents are, how many brothers and sisters, uncles and aunts, how many cows you've milked . . ."

"All right!" Renee exclaimed, laughing out loud. "First of all, I've never milked any cows. You've got me beat hands down on that one—no pun intended. There aren't too many cows in Tucson, which kind of makes it hard to learn. I have one brother, who still lives there, my parents too. They think the sun rises and sets only in the desert and I happen to disagree with them completely. As soon as I saw California, I knew that's where I had to be."

"And you've been there since . . ."

"Since I graduated from college," Renee finished. "My parents still wish I'd come back to Tucson but they've gradually stopped bugging me about it. Especially since I've been in Long Beach for almost six years."

Greg seemed satisfied with her brief autobiography and for a few minutes they strolled on in silence. Finally Greg said, "So, Miss Michaelson, just what are you doing here in glorious Waikiki with only a girlfriend to keep you company?"

Renee glanced at him in surprise. "What's so wrong with being with a girlfriend?"

Greg smiled. "Nothing. I just supposed . . . I don't know, I just thought perhaps you would have been with . . . whomever you were involved with." His smile faded and Renee noted a serious glint flash within the grass-green gaze. "Are you?"

"What?"

"Involved with someone?"

Renee dropped her gaze and glanced down at the pavement. Despite the foolishness of it, she felt herself flushing. She hadn't expected a question like that. She didn't really like it either. Not at this point. "No," she answered impulsively. "You?"

"Nope." He appeared to relax, as if her answer had satisfied his curiosity about a matter that had been bothering him.

But as they continued the long walk back to their hotels, chatting and discussing details of each other's work, a part of Renee's mind was wandering in another direction. His question earlier was really niggling at her. But what was she more disturbed about, the question itself or her answer? Now, that was ridiculous—why should she be getting uptight about it? So she had lied about it, what difference did that make? It just made things simpler, that was all. And she had seen the look of relief on Greg's face when she'd said she wasn't involved with anyone. That should be enough to convince her she had done the right thing. It was obviously what he wanted to hear, so why should she have said something that may very well have spoiled the rest of the evening? But still, to be honest, she wasn't too comfortable with the answer herself. It had opened up that same old bag of worms she was more than a little tired of wrestling with.

Shaking aside the uncomfortable feeling, Renee drew her attention back to what Greg was saying. "That wasn't such a long walk after all."

Renee looked around her in surprise; they were already standing in front of her hotel. The street was noisy and crowded with the nighttime traffic, but she only now noticed it. "I can't believe we're back here already."

Greg smiled, a slow, gorgeous smile that further enhanced his handsome face. "Are you feeling any better?"

Renee frowned. "What . . ."

"Your stomach."

She laughed and played with a lock of hair that brushed just above her shoulder. "Much. Walking was just what I needed."

There was a silence between them for a moment and Renee felt a little uncomfortable. Then suddenly Greg took her hand in his and said, "Are you tired?"

She wasn't, but for some reason she didn't want to

do anything else tonight; so far so good, and she didn't want to do anything that might mar the enjoyable evening.

"Sort of," she fibbed.

Greg chewed his bottom lip thoughtfully and looked at her consideringly. Then he tugged gently on her hand and said, "C'mere. Just for a minute."

She followed behind, her steps moving twice as fast as his to keep up with his long stride. He led her around the corner, brushing hurriedly past strolling pedestrians, then shocking Renee as he suddenly disappeared around an obscured corner, pulling her with him. They were in a narrow, dimly lit alleyway; Renee's eyes had trouble adjusting to the darkness.

"Greg, what are you doing?" she said anxiously. "What are we doing here?"

"Shhh," he cautioned her, pulling her rapidly against his chest and placing both arms around her tightly.

Renee's concern over the sinister surroundings was quickly overshadowed in light of the unexpected nearness of Greg's body to hers. No matter that they'd spent hours in each other's company, had danced together earlier at least this close. This was different, entirely different.

"I saw no reason to make a spectacle of ourselves in public," Greg explained.

"But we weren't . . ."

"We will be." He gathered his arms around her even tighter and lowered his head to hers. Renee's gaze, which had adjusted somewhat by now to the darkness, took in his shadowed features. His expression held an intensity that startled her, sending shivers of expectation along her spine.

Slowly, determinedly, his lips descended upon hers, resting gently on them for a moment, then coaxing them into willing submission. The utter sweetness, the soundless question in his manner, touched her deeply.

As such, she was helpless to do anything but respond to this provocation. Parting her own soft lips, she felt the velvet roughness of his tongue sweep across her teeth, then carefully, thoroughly search the inner recesses of her mouth. Something warm and tingly urged her even closer to him, and as she did so, one leg bent slightly at the knee, the other nudged firmly against his thigh. All of her senses were keen now, the heat of his nearness alighting her nervous system with a fiery response.

Somewhere in the deeper, more questioning recesses of her brain a question badgered at her, a question that, strangely, troubled her greatly. Was it simply that she had never experienced this sort of kiss with Louis, or that she had completely forgotten? She'd always known a certain satisfaction when Louis kissed her, of course, but this . . . this was a genuine kiss! She'd never experienced the depth of feeling, the sheer desire, Greg was provoking within her now. Her hands seemed to have a mind of their own; she was hardly aware of them slipping beneath his jacket, kneading the solid contours of his back, her thumbs sliding sensuously up his spinal column.

At some point—it seemed like hours later—Greg eased his mouth away from hers, trailing whisper-soft kisses along her face and forehead before coming to rest on the crown of her head. Renee's chin lay against his collarbone and she drew in a deep, calming breath. Greg placed his hands on her shoulders and she looked up at him, wondering if he noticed the deep flush in her cheeks. She bit her lower lip shyly as a tiny smile curled her burnished lips. She was at a total loss for words, but Greg seemed not to be disturbed in the least by her discomfort.

He merely gazed down at her with those hypnotic, grass-green eyes, which in the darkened alleyway took on an almost translucent glow. Finally he spoke, and Renee could only marvel at the levity of his tone. She could barely find the strength to speak.

"When do you get up in the morning?" he asked. Not what are you doing, can I see you, just, when do you get up.

Renee shrugged. "I've been waking up around six thirty or seven." At the amused look on his face, she added somewhat sheepishly, "I can't help it. Too much practice."

"Early is fine with me too. My hotel has an unbelievable breakfast buffet. Why don't you meet me there at seven thirty?"

Breakfast was Renee's absolute favorite meal of the day, and her face lit up enthusiastically. But since she'd been declining Marcy's touring and exploring expeditions, leaving the two of them apart most of the day, she'd settled on room service almost every day since she'd been here.

"I'd love it," she agreed. She pulled back and fluffed out her hair as she glanced around them. Amazingly, they were still alone. "Greg, this place is kind of spooky. Let's get out of here."

Greg laughed and put an arm around her shoulders, leading her back onto the sidewalk. "Pretty damned convenient too," he muttered, and Renee had to chuckle. That it was.

They covered the distance to Renee's hotel lobby quickly and Greg gave her one last peck on the cheek before he joined the stream of night pedestrians and continued on toward his hotel. Renee watched him go, then turned and headed toward the elevators.

She punched the Up arrow with a bit of flourish, and began to pace with a lightened step as she waited for the elevator. Yes, she decided, this is definitely what the doctor ordered. Indeed, it was becoming a rather pleasant diversion to ponder upon what Louis, with his double standard and chauvinistic attitude, would think about this.

CHAPTER THREE

Renee had the blow dryer going full blast when Marcy stumbled into the dressing area of the room. One side of her face was creased by the pillow and her hair looked as if she'd just come in out of a ferocious windstorm. Renee was busy lifting sections of her hair with one hand, keeping the dryer moving in an up-and-down motion with the other. She grinned at Marcy's image which suddenly appeared in the mirror.

"God, you look atrocious," she commented, raising her voice above the steady drone of the dryer.

Marcy shoved back a heavy lock and yawned widely, peering at Renee through barely opened eyes. "What's going on, Michaelson?" she asked in a raspy voice. "What the hell time is it anyway?"

"It's seven, that's what the hell time it is."

"Seven!" Marcy groaned. "Come on, when are you gonna wake up at a decent hour?"

"It's decent the rest of the year, why shouldn't it be now?"

Marcy shook her head slowly and rubbed her forehead. She turned and lumbered back to the bed, sitting down heavily on the edge and resting her head in the palms of her hands. "God, I'll never wake up." With another groan she slid slowly back onto the pillow and threw her arms over her face.

Renee, finished with the drying, walked into the bedroom, observing her friend as she twisted the cord around the handle. "What's the matter with you? Looks like your party last night was a success."

Marcy moaned in response and turned onto her side. "Success or not, I don't think I'll ever make it out of this bed."

"Then don't. You've been running around like a madwoman ever since we got here." She had indeed. Marcy was an explorer if ever there was one. She made friends easily, too, so just because the two of them only saw each other at bedtime didn't mean Marcy was hurting for company.

Apparently Marcy fell asleep again, for she remained silent as Renee finished dressing. By the time Renee let herself out the door, the girl was snoring lightly and Renee smiled to herself as she walked down the corridor to the elevators.

She walked the couple of blocks to the hotel Greg was staying at with an unmistakable briskness in her step. The ocean breeze felt marvelously good, lifting and fluffing out her light-brown hair. She breathed in deeply, listening to the distant, steady rhythm of the waves breaking on the beach. The streets weren't as crowded at this time of day, and Renee was glad they'd agreed to meet early. Her footsteps quickened as she approached the front entrance of the hotel.

Greg was standing at the registration desk, talking with a clerk. Renee smiled. Had he been a little shorter, and she a little taller, they could have passed for the Bobbsey twins. She had worn a pair of white walking shorts with a tomato red cap-sleeved blouse and a pair of white ankle strap sandals. Greg was wearing white shorts also, though his were a little more abbreviated than her own, and the polo shirt he wore was bright red.

Renee placed her hands on her hips, swinging her tiny shoulder bag behind her. Finishing his business with the clerk, Greg turned to see her grinning with obvious amusement as her gaze swept him from head to toe. Then he noticed the source of her amusement and a wide grin broke across his face.

"Tell me something, Greg Daniels, do you have ESP?"

"I could ask you the same thing, couldn't I?"

"Should I go back and change, or would you care to?"

Greg shrugged and spread one hand outward. "Whatever for?"

Renee grimaced with obvious disdain. "Come *on.* We look like a pair of middle-aged married tourists."

Greg laughed at her apt description. "Not really," he said, shaking his head and glancing down. "Our shoes are different." He was wearing a pair of blue and white running shoes.

Renee looked down at her sandals and cocked an eyebrow. "Yeah. I guess you're right."

Greg stepped forward and took her arm. "Are you hungry?"

"Starved."

"Then let's get after it."

Inside the main restaurant Renee was astounded by the sight of a thirty-foot-long buffet table overflowing with the most bountiful, exotic assortment of foods she'd ever seen in one place at the same time. The serving plates, they discovered quickly, were not nearly large enough for the assortment of fruits and cheeses and breads and pastries and egg dishes. Renee's eyes were larger than her stomach and her plate was heaped as high as Greg's by the time they made it back to the table.

"One thing I've always liked," Greg said as they placed napkins over their laps and picked up knives and forks. "A woman with a healthy appetite."

Renee frowned self-deprecatingly. "I don't know if 'healthy' is the term for it. Gluttonous might be more like it."

Nevertheless she finished off more of the king-size breakfast than she expected to. Finally, though, she had to give up. Greg was still busy with his plate as Renee sipped her coffee, inwardly amazed at the incredible change in her dietary habits. In one day she had gone from an almost constant state of fasting to gorging herself on an enormous dinner and breakfast.

"When are you leaving?" Greg asked. Renee set her cup down and shook her head.

"You know I almost forgot that we're leaving so soon. Day after tomorrow. How about you?"

"We don't leave until Monday."

Renee sighed. "Must be nice." She hesitated then added, "We?"

"I was referring to Robert Simpson, a good friend of mine. We've made this trip several times over the years."

Frowning, Renee suddenly remembered something. "Is . . . was that who you were looking for yesterday on the beach? When you kicked sand all over me?" Her eyes conveyed a teasing gleam and Greg smiled back at her.

"Uh-huh. But I forgot all about him soon enough, didn't I?"

Renee blushed prettily and Greg suddenly pushed his plate back and wiped his mouth with his napkin. "Listen, have you seen any of the other islands while you've been here?"

Renee shook her head. "Marcy and I couldn't come to an agreement on which one to include in our package deal, so we decided to just stay here the whole time." She shrugged. "It was cheaper too."

"But it really would be a shame not to see *anything* else but Oahu." Greg rubbed his chin thoughtfully. "How would you like to go with me to Maui tomorrow?"

Renee's mouth parted slightly, then she said, "Oh, I didn't know you were leaving. Are you staying there until Monday?"

Greg shook his head. "No. It's just an impulsive thought. I have connections in Lahaina. It's the one island I've never visited and since you've never been there, I thought perhaps this would be a good opportunity for both of us."

Renee picked up her cup, brought it to her lips,

and sipped thoughtfully. Her mind was spinning a mile a minute as she struggled with the surprising invitation he'd just thrown out. Greg signaled the waiter to refill their cups and a few moments passed before he pressed her for an answer.

"Well?" His eyebrows rose in curiosity. "Does the idea appeal to you or not?"

Renee laughed nervously. "Sure it appeals to me. I'd love to see Maui. I . . . but, there wouldn't really be enough time."

"Why not?"

"Like I said, we leave day after tomorrow."

"What time? Morning? Evening?"

"Three o'clock in the afternoon."

Greg gestured with both hands palm upward. "No problem. We could have the whole day Friday and come back early Saturday morning."

Renee held her breath for a moment then expelled it slowly. She stared blankly out the window near them, contemplating the whole situation. The fact of the matter was she'd *love* to see Maui. Honolulu was fun, but the idea of seeing another of the Hawaiian islands appealed to her immensely. And Greg was certainly nice enough a companion to go with. Nice enough! What an understatement. He was charming, friendly, sexy as . . .

Then what was the problem? The answer of course was the face which hovered, as always, not far from her thoughts; Louis's face. How could she do something like going off with another man when she was still in love with Louis? A date was one thing; to stay overnight with the man was something else altogether. But then, she'd already taken a step in that direction, hadn't she? She was suddenly acutely aware of the memory of last night's kiss with Greg; she actually trembled just thinking of it. Then she thought of Louis again, what he would do in the same situation. She was somehow certain Louis had had his share of kisses while away . . . if not a great deal more. The thought of it, the likelihood of it, filled her with the same old vengeful rage she'd succumbed to yesterday. Suddenly Greg's proposition didn't seem so out-of-the-question. As a matter of fact, it sounded damned good.

"Hey," Greg said, snapping his fingers in front of her face. "Come back to earth."

Renee's stare broke and she turned to him with a smile. "I'm sorry. I was just thinking."

"That was obvious enough."

She cocked her head to one side and held his gaze for a moment. "Yes."

"Yes what?"

"Yes, I'd love to go with you to Maui."

Greg smiled a slow, totally gratified grin, then reached across the table to pick up her hand. "I'm sure glad you said that." His thumb caressed her inner wrist and his green eyes danced with expectation.

Glancing at his watch suddenly, he said, "Tell you what. I need to make a few phone calls if we're gonna get this show on the road. Would you like to come with me or meet me later?"

Renee looked indecisive for a moment. "Well, I probably should check on Marcy and let her know I'm going."

"All right. Meet me for lunch at Simone's?"

Renee stared at him in disbelief. "Greg! After all this? If I keep this up, I'm gonna waddle onto the plane Saturday."

Greg reached for his wallet and scoffed. "I'd rather see you waddle than blow away the next time a stiff breeze picks up."

Renee's laugh was not without a certain degree of pleasure. She couldn't imagine Louis ever having implied that she was actually *skinny.* He was too busy focusing on what he referred to as her "excess baggage." *Start getting used to those couple of pounds, Renee, and before you know it they'll turn into ten.* Many were the times she'd had to endure painful, envious sessions as he forked mouthfuls of juicy tenderloin while she toyed with a lone stalk of broccoli.

They walked quickly to Renee's hotel and she bid him good-bye until later that afternoon. Marcy was still sprawled out on her bed when Renee let herself in. She quietly made her way across the darkened room, waiting until she reached the dressing area before switching on the light.

The motion, however, wakened her friend. "What's going on?" Marcy mumbled from beneath the covers. Renee stepped back into the room and sat down on her own bed.

"Are you feeling human yet?"

Marcy groaned and pulled herself to an upright position. She yawned and rubbed her face, then shoved back a mass of hair. Her eyes opened wider as she looked Renee over. "You look chipper this morning. What are you doing back so soon?"

"Well, I came back to discuss something with you. What are you doing tomorrow?"

"Hopefully not the same thing I'm doing today." Marcy frowned. "Why?"

Renee studied her nails as she answered as casually as possible. "I . . . I'm not going to be around, that's all. I thought perhaps I should tell you in case you needed me."

"Needed you? For what? We haven't even seen each other except—" Marcy's eyes narrowed. "Hey, what's going on? What are you up to?"

Renee took in a deep breath and let it out quickly. "I'm . . . we're . . . oh, what the heck. I'm going to Maui with Greg tomorrow," she blurted out. "He promised to have me back by Saturday morning, which should give us plenty of time to pack and be at the airport by three o'clock."

Marcy said nothing, merely stared disbelievingly at her friend. "You're kidding," she said flatly.

Renee shrugged. "No. I'm not." Suddenly she hopped off the bed and pulled her suitcase out from beneath. "I might as well start packing while I'm here. I'm supposed to meet Greg for lunch at Simone's."

Marcy swung her legs over the side of her bed and watched Renee thoughtfully for a moment. "Y'know something. I'm afraid to say anything. I'm afraid it might break the spell. Never, *ever* did I think I'd see the day when Renee Michaelson would come to her senses, get off her duff, and quit thinking about the high and mighty Louis Mandol."

Renee opened her mouth to say something, but

Marcy held up one hand to silence her. "Nope. Don't say anything. This is none of my business, so I won't offer any more of my personal feelings on the subject."

Renee was grateful for that, but she couldn't help noticing the smug smile on Marcy's face as she left the room. Renee continued her packing as Marcy took a long shower.

Finished, she walked to the window and drew on the cord to pull back the curtain. Absently, she crossed her arms over her chest and stared out across the downtown Honolulu skyline.

Was that what she'd done? Gotten off her duff and forgotten about Louis? In a certain sense she supposed she had. But not in the way Marcy was thinking, although she'd let her go on thinking it if it made her happy.

No, Louis was very much a part of her thoughts, even now. She'd loved him for an entire year, and still refused to believe that an emotion as strong as love could be diminished by a temporary separation, regardless of how much she hadn't wanted it. Perhaps it was time to look at the whole thing a little more philosophically, she'd finally convinced herself. If Louis need time away from her, needed to spread his wings a little, well, then, there was nothing she could do about it. Besides, maybe she needed a little of the same. An overjustification perhaps? Well, it was her only defense about a situation over which she had very little control.

Greg's offer of an "island" rendezvous might be just the thing to help her accept Louis's indiscretions a little easier—to even the score so to speak. It was the ideal situation really. She needed Greg at this point in her life, and obviously he needed her. And it was a temporary situation, which was all for the better. No commitments, no problems.

CHAPTER FOUR

The airplane banked sharply to the left and Renee leaned her face closer to the window. "It's beautiful," she commented, taking in the lush verdancy of the island of Maui. "The water's so blue. Green too."

"You'll love it," Greg said, placing his copy of a flight magazine back in the seat pocket ahead of him.

As the airplane slowly lost altitude Renee soaked up the details of the beautiful island—white, sandy beaches, acres of tall, swaying sugar cane, jagged, cloud-crowned mountain peaks.

The landing was smooth, the temperature perfect, and by the time they were in the "taxi," a worn, American station wagon, Renee was filled with excitement and self-satisfaction over her decision in coming. She regretted only that she and Marcy had restricted their visit to Oahu. Honolulu was charming and romantic in its own right, but Maui had a distinction altogether different and interesting. In no time, it seemed, the driver was pulling up in front of their hotel in Lahaina. Renee and Greg walked behind the driver as he took their luggage into the lobby. She half expected to meet Greg's old friend who was presently hotel manager of the resort complex. But apparently he wasn't around and in a matter of minutes they had checked in and were standing at the door of their room. Greg's friend had been kind enough to accommodate them with a room with a magnificent view of the Pacific through a perfect frame of gently swaying palm trees.

A lush assortment of other tropical plants and fragrant flowers grew in tamed abandon in the small courtyard conjoining their room's small patio. It was remarkably different from the high-rise hotel that she and Marcy were staying at in Waikiki. The stuff that honeymoons were made of, she added rather wistfully. . . .

Greg tipped the bellhop and turned to her. "Well, do you like it?"

"Are you kidding? It's gorgeous!" And it was, Renee thought. *This* was what Hawaii was all about.

She turned and followed Greg into the room, but after only a few steps, she stopped dead in her tracks. Greg had opened the sliding glass patio doors and was placing their luggage on the baggage rack, talking to her all the while. Renee didn't hear a single word of what he was saying. Inexplicably, she felt as though she had walked straight into an invisible barrier.

She gulped spasmodically and forced her gaze around the spacious room. It was large, bright, cheery—all the things one could ask for in a resort hotel. But what did any of this have to do with her? She looked across the room at Greg and saw a man, a tall, very handsome, virile man but a stranger all the same.

Good God, what was she doing here? She didn't know this man, not really. They had met only two days before. The gravity of what she had done—what she was about to do—was blatantly pointed out by the huge, king-size bed positioned in the center of the room. Reality hit her with the force of a bucket of cold water. A strange sense of disorientation, stronger than any she had ever experienced, seized her and unknowingly her features acquired a tense, pained expression.

"Renee? Is something wrong? If you don't like it, we can . . ." Greg was studying her discontented face with a frown.

"Wha—No, no . . . it's fine. I"—Renee shook her head and forced a smile—"I was just trying to remember something." She turned and snatched up her purse, fumbled through it for a moment, and withdrew a colorful brochure. "Here it is." She sat down in the chair nearest the window and said, "I read this last night." She gestured with the small, folded paper she had removed from her purse. "It's a brochure on Maui. Did you know that Wailuku isn't the original capital of the island?"

"Uh, yeah." Greg sounded vague, obviously puzzled by this rather odd turn of conversation. He opened his suitcase and began extracting a few items. "What was the name of the old one, Hana, Hanu . . ."

"Hana," Renee said. "Here, listen to this." She

read a descriptive paragraph or two from the brochure, and then looked up at him. "Greg?"

"Hmmm?"

"I have an idea. I mean, I think it would be a good one, that is, if you didn't have any other specific plans for the day. Did you?"

"No, not really." He sat down on the edge of the bed and looked at her curiously.

Renee leaned forward in her chair. "Then let's go there. To Hana. I'd love to see what it must have been like years ago, when the island was young. I don't think I've ever gotten over Michener's *Hawaii.*" That was the truth, although it was a very small part of the reason for her suggestion. The truth was, she desperately needed to get out of there, to regain her composure and sense of security. And there was no way that was going to happen in this room, not now at least.

Greg smiled wryly at her. "I've never been there myself. I guess if you really want to—"

"Oh, good! It's only thirty-something miles. We could rent a car and drive there." She could just hear what Marcy would have to say about this sudden exploring urge.

"I guess we could." Greg hesitated and snapped shut his suitcase. He glanced at his watch. "It's only ten thirty. We've got enough time."

Renee smiled as much in relief as enthusiasm. "Great!" The smile faded slightly as she raised her brows and said, "But I guess I should mention—there is another famous scenic spot here on the island. I don't know. Maybe you'd rather go there."

"Where?"

"Charles Lindbergh's grave."

Greg grimaced and said dryly, "I think I'll skip on that one."

"It's supposed to be really beautiful."

"Just the same, I'm not too eager to drive halfway across an island just to look at a grave."

"All right then," Renee said, smiling again. "Hana it is." She stood then and walked to the vanity in the dressing area. Taking out her brush from her purse, she held it mid-air and said, "Just let me freshen up a bit. I'll be ready in a few minutes."

By the time they were heading away from the rental car lot in a compact-size car, Renee's former frame of mind gradually reasserted itself. The scenery they were traveling through was simply too lush, too breathtakingly beautiful, to focus one's attention on anything less. She and Greg chatted easily about a variety of subjects—politics, favorite football teams, the economy. And though they didn't agree on everything, Renee welcomed the stimulating banter as it pulled her attention even further from the situation she'd gotten herself in. She *had* done the right thing, she reassured herself, in deciding to come along with Greg on this trip. If nothing else, she could at least have the pleasure of saying she had seen something of Hawaii besides a hotel room and a crowded beach.

This, indeed, was a far cry from that scene. As the highway they were traveling gradually ascended into the dense, verdurous mountains, the wide span of white beach below extended endlessly, contrasting sharply with the vivid blue-green of the Pacific. What an absolute paradise, Renee thought. Now why should she feel this pang in her stomach, feel as though she shouldn't really be enjoying it this much? The answer eluded her, and determinedly, she forced the inexplicable sentiment aside.

But paradise, she soon discovered, wasn't without its problems. The highway diminished into little more than a two-lane, sometimes one-lane road. As they climbed even higher into the mountains, formerly gentle curves were rapidly becoming twisting, hairpin turns that soon had Renee on the edge of her seat, but for more reasons than the hazardous driving conditions. She kept her face turned to look out the window, afraid that if Greg saw her face he would certainly laugh. She had to be green at the gills the way her stomach was churning around inside.

The higher they ascended, the sharper the turns and the worse she felt. She was unaware that she had moaned until Greg asked with obvious concern, "Renee? Are you all right?"

She bobbed her head up and down, afraid to open her mouth and speak. She was getting sicker and sicker by the second. Suddenly she couldn't hold her head up anymore and slumped down, leaning back against the headrest, shutting her eyes tightly and grimacing. She didn't care what Greg thought by now.

"Renee, what is it? What's wrong?" Greg insisted. "You look terrible."

"G-getting sick," Renee muttered.

"It's all right. Just hold on. Can you?" Greg's eyes shifted rapidly from Renee to the hazardous twisting mountain road. Incredibly, the thirty-mile journey had already stretched into two and a half hours.

Renee nodded in answer to his question and didn't open her eyes until she felt the car come to a stop. Greg had parked on a scenic overlook and had already hopped out and come around to open her door.

"Here, I'll help you," he said, reaching in and taking her by the hand.

Renee's legs were so weak they wobbled and she clung to Greg's arm as she stood next to the car door. But the breeze was refreshingly cool this high up and instinctively she took in a deep breath of it. It cleared her head a little and she glanced sheepishly at Greg.

"I must look like the biggest baby you've ever seen."

Greg's expression, however, was devoid of any amusement. His green gaze studied her with worried concern and suddenly Renee felt bad that she had alarmed him so.

"You don't look like a baby to me at all," he said. "But you do look sick. Are you feeling any better?"

"Uh-huh." Renee nodded and drew in another deep breath. "Let's walk around some."

Greg placed an arm securely around her shoulders as he slowly led her to the rail at the edge of the overlook. Renee was regaining her sense of equilibrium and her upset stomach was finally beginning to settle down.

"Greg," she said softly. "I'm really sorry."

"What for? You can't help it if you get sick."

Renee's gaze scanned the sheer drop below, the shimmering white beach and aquamarine ocean lapping the shoreline. "Yes, but I shouldn't have talked you into this."

"Would you stop talking nonsense?" Greg sounded perturbed now, and as Renee looked up at him, she could see that he really was. The breeze whipped his hair back from his forehead and she was struck, as she had been on first seeing him, with his incredible handsomeness. But his eyes! Their rich verdancy was flecked with the azure of the cloudless sky, lending them a deep turquoise brilliance. More impressive, however, than their color was the genuine concern they reflected. Renee realized at that point, with unquestionable certainty, that he really cared about her very much. She felt a flip-flop sensation within and she swallowed deeply, averting her eyes.

"I'm not talking nonsense," she answered. "I should have known when I read the map that I might get sick. But I didn't think 'hairpin' turns would be quite so dramatic."

"Do you mean you suffer from carsickness?" Greg looked at her in surprise.

Renee grimaced self-derisively as she nodded. "I didn't think I still could get it. We shouldn't have come. I'm sorry. Really."

Suddenly Greg burst out laughing, a rich, hearty sound. Then he placed one arm around her and hugged her to him tightly. "It's not that serious, and anyway you're forgiven," he said, still smiling. "The only thing is, what are we gonna do now? We're only halfway there and these curves continue most of the way up. Do you want to go back?"

Renee frowned and shook her head. "That would be such a waste. And I'll probably get sick that way too." She hesitated and chewed thoughtfully on her forefinger. "There is one thing that might help."

"What?"

"Let me take the wheel."

Greg nodded slowly. "Hmmm. You're right. That would probably help."

Renee turned, thinking he was of the same mind she was, to start back for the car. But Greg blocked her path and she looked up at him questioningly.

"Do you feel better now?"

"Oh, yes. Much."

"Good enough for this?" He grasped her by the shoulders and pulled her to him, pressing his lips against hers.

And indeed, she really did feel better! Immensely better. She swayed against him automatically, wanting . . . needing the sensations his lips and mouth and tongue were bringing her. She responded mindlessly, kissing him back with a fervency that matched his own, the confusion and doubts over what she was doing here completely forgotten and totally unimportant.

All that was significant now were the arms that bound her so closely, the lips that crushed hers so relentlessly, eliciting a yearning within her like none other she'd ever known. This *was* paradise, she decided. What difference did it matter if she was sharing it with the wrong man? All that mattered was the moment, the sensation, the fantasy that he *was* the right man and that he fulfilled the fantasy so perfectly.

Renee was practically breathless when finally Greg released her. Disconcerted, she bit her lower lip and ran her fingers through her breeze-tossed hair. Greg was staring down at her, but she wasn't up to facing the intensity of those deep aqua eyes. She had already absorbed enough of that in his kiss, a kiss she somehow knew that he did not bestow too often, or too easily. But the knowledge of this only intensified her discomfort.

"Ready to go?" she asked lightly, turning to walk back to the car. Greg did not follow her immediately, but when he finally did return to the car, it was obvious that he too had had a difficult time in regaining his composure.

The sun was past its highest pinnacle by the time they reached Hana. Driving had helped Renee immensely; she was not, however, looking forward to the long return drive, though she knew she must if she wanted to avoid carsickness.

Stepping out of the car, she found she was slightly weary from the long journey. The scenery awaiting them, however, quickly restored her enthusiasm. If she'd thought the scenic overlook was paradise, this was absolute heaven. Her own images from scenes in Michener's *Hawaii* could not have matched any better the sweet tropical beauty that surrounded them, the deeply bronzed, natural beauty of some of the few remaining pure-Hawaiian villagers.

Her appetite wasn't suffering either by now, she quickly discovered. She and Greg lunched inside the tiny village's only restaurant, enjoying the refreshing breeze wafting through the screened windows, the peaceful contentment of only nature's sounds surrounding them.

Greg pushed his empty plate back, took a long sip of his iced tea, then set his glass down and shook his head. His green eyes glinted with amusement and Renee frowned as she tilted her head to one side. "What are you looking at me like that for?"

"Like what?" Greg asked innocently.

Renee's gaze narrowed. "You know very well what I mean. Like you're laughing at me or something."

Greg chuckled, stretched his arms straight up and back, then clasped them behind his head. "I'm just wondering what other weird things about you I've yet to find out. Y'know, did you ever consider that those blue contact lenses might be the cause of your carsickness?"

Renee clucked her tongue and rolled her brown eyes. "I *knew* I shouldn't have mentioned that. Here, I'll show you, since you're having such a hard time believing me." Suddenly she lifted a hand to her cheek and with the barest blink of her right eye a blue lense popped out of her eye and into the palm of her hand. Stretching out her arm, she held it out for his inspection. "See, my eyes are still brown."

Greg's gaze took in the single blue lense, then, as his arms came down to his sides, he practically gaped at Renee in astonishment.

"How in the hell did you do that?"

It was Renee's turn to chuckle and almost as quickly as she had taken the lense out she popped it back into her eye.

Greg squinted and flinched visibly. "Christ! How do you do that? It hurts just to watch. I thought you needed a mirror to look into."

"As easy as milkin' cows," Renee answered glibly. She leaned forward across the table and said in a low, conspiratorial tone, "Know what else I can do? I can sit in a lotus position, crisscross my arms around my back and grab my opposite big toes." She pushed her chair back against the wooden floor, half-stood, and said eagerly, "Want to see?"

"Sit down," Greg ordered gruffly, though his eyes were laughing.

Renee's eyes widened in feigned innocence. "You wanted to know if there was anything else weird about me, so I . . ."

"Okay, okay." Greg leaned one elbow on the table and propped his chin in the palm of his hand. "You know, this has got to be the silliest lunchtime discussion I've ever had." He paused, wiggled his eyebrows, and said, "But it sure beat the hell out of talking business."

Renee agreed thoroughly; how long had it been since she'd even attempted to act so silly, let alone get away with it? How was it that she felt so free, so uninhibited with a man she had only met a couple of days ago? She hadn't thought such a thing was possible; it certainly hadn't been the case with Louis, that was for sure. But, gosh, she felt so much herself—the real Renee. It felt so *good* not to be worried about whether or not she was behaving like a lady in public, saying the right things, certainly never engaging in anything so gauche as removing her contact lenses just for the fun of it, or getting ready to do her famous yoga position. And she would have done it, right there next to the table! Why couldn't Louis loosen up like this man? It could make things so much more enjoyable, relaxing . . . To heck with it, she wasn't going to waste one more precious minute of this marvelous day letting her thoughts ramble in *that* direction. And she didn't.

The trip back didn't seem nearly as long and Renee negotiated the hairpin turns a good deal easier this time. But by the time they arrived at the hotel, she had reached a state of contented exhaustion.

As she opened the car door, she just sat there, too weary to move.

"I'll never make it to the room," she groaned, and Greg chuckled lightly. He got out of the car and came around to help her out.

"C'mon, what have you done today? Get out of the car, you lazy bum."

Renee opened her eyes and shot him a derisive look. "*Me,* lazy? That's easy enough for you to say when all you did was lean out the window and take a bunch of pictures."

"Wait till you see them," Greg defended himself, "you'll be glad one of us took some."

Renee sighed, got out of the car, and walked automatically alongside him, her eyelids drooping heavily. Entering their hotel room, the memory of how she had felt upon leaving it earlier today did not enter her mind. She plopped down heavily on the bed and kicked off her sandals.

"You look sleepy, kiddo," Greg said, unstrapping his elaborate camera gear and placing it carefully on the dresser.

With another long sigh Renee fell back onto the

pillow and closed her eyes. "Do you mind if I take a little nap?"

"Go ahead. Don't forget, though, we're having dinner at eight. I want you to meet Steve."

Renee nodded. She couldn't care less at this point about having dinner, period. She rolled onto her side and within seconds was sleeping soundly.

"I hope you two are enjoying the place," Steve Henson said. Greg's amiable, boyish-faced college friend had just sat down to join them, and Greg had introduced him to Renee.

"The hotel is fantastic," Greg assured him. "You're doing a great job."

Renee nodded her agreement. "The food is absolutely marvelous too. Compliments to your chef."

Steve appeared gratified by their sincere comments and chatted with them a while longer before standing. "Listen, you two, I've really enjoyed it. But I'm afraid I'm back on duty now."

"Tsk. Tsk." Greg chuckled. "Is this the same carefree, irresponsible Steve Henson I went to college with?"

Steve smiled wryly. "The very same I'm afraid. Old age has made a workaholic out of me."

Greg stood and shook Steve's hand. "Thanks for everything, old buddy. I'll see you tomorrow before we leave."

"Great. Very nice to have met you, Renee."

"The pleasure was mine," Renee returned, smiling. After he'd walked away she commented, "He's really a super guy."

"Sure is," Greg agreed. He shook his head. "It's

hard to believe it's been eight years since I've seen him."

"Hmmm. Eight years. Let's see, that's twenty-two, twenty-three plus eight. That makes you, what? Thirty, thirty-one years old?"

Greg tossed his head back and laughed. "Ah, such a flatterer. No, I was a few years ahead of Steve. I'll be thirty-seven on my next big one."

Renee looked surprised. "You're kidding."

"No, I'm not. And please, don't try to tell me I look like a kid."

"I wouldn't go *that* far." Her eyes narrowed as she leveled him an appraising look. "Hmmm. Yeah, I guess I see what you mean. There is that rather deep groove along the side of—"

"On the other hand, I think I'll take the kid," he interrupted wryly. It was his turn to cast her a scrutinizing look, but Renee intercepted it before he made any comment.

"Don't ask. Twenty-seven on my next birthday."

"Which is?"

"October. Just a few months away."

"Libra?"

"Mmm-hmm."

Greg lifted his glass in salute. "From one Libra to another."

Renee saluted in return and after downing the rest of her wine agreed to Greg's suggestion that they have another. She was having a marvelous time. She felt completely at ease with Greg now, had enjoyed the day far more than she'd expected to, and was relishing the nerve-soothing effects of the wine and the relaxing atmosphere of the restaurant.

By the time Greg suggested they return to the room, Renee was beyond any further questioning of her motives or the sensibility of the entire situation. She'd known from the start what she'd gotten into and by now rather felt an obligation to go ahead with it. She owed it to herself, and as she'd already decided, this little experience would even the score with Louis quite nicely.

"Little experience," however, turned out to be a ridiculous understatement, Renee was to later reflect. The night turned out to be one of the most memorable in her life. The day's adventure, of course, had certainly helped things along. Such intense togetherness had resulted in Renee's feeling that somehow she knew Greg as well as she knew Louis, though the differences in personalities of the two men were like night and day. Greg was totally open with her in both his opinions and his feelings, a trait Renee found particularly engaging, especially as she was used to dealing with a man who kept her guessing almost constantly about his own emotions. Indeed, she had almost come to believe it was an impossibility for a man to be so expressive.

"Would you care to watch television?" Greg asked as he opened the door and she entered ahead of him.

"Only if you—" Renee's answer was cut short as she turned and saw him standing mere inches from her. His green gaze was steady and piercing, making his question nothing more than a formality. Renee swallowed spasmodically, acutely aware of a terrifically strong pull toward this man she had known for such a short length of time, yet who had somehow managed to secure her complete trust.

He moved even closer to her and rested his hands lightly on her shoulders. "Actually, I couldn't care less about it," he said in a low tone.

Renee felt a shudder course through her and instinctively she tilted her head backward. She closed her eyes, immediately feeling Greg's lips upon hers, warm and moist and hinting faintly of the wine they'd shared. Her own lips were willing, and she opened her mouth to his, inviting his tongue as it brushed lightly against her teeth, playing against her own, then reaching farther into the deeper recesses of her mouth.

Her insides felt warm and liquid as his hands traveled slowly down her back, stroking and massaging, sliding downward to rest atop her buttocks. She brought her own hands up, working them in tiny circles against the hard musculature of his trim waist. When he groaned once at her touch and pulled away suddenly, her eyes flew open in surprise. What had happened? Why was he turning on his heel and walking away from her? But as he switched off the ceiling light, leaving the lamp on the vanity still burning, she quickly realized his intention. He walked back to her, and, taking her by the hand, led her to the wide bed.

He sat down on the edge of it and positioned her securely between his thighs, their solid contour rock-hard against her own. Instinctively she longed to reach up and run her fingers through his hair, press her hands along the ridge of his broad shoulders. Yet something in his demeanor bid her to refrain just yet, so she stood perfectly still within his grasp, unaware that she was barely breathing as his fingers reached up to the top button of her blouse.

Carefully he undid them all and as the cotton top slid off her shoulders with tantalizing slowness Renee shivered beneath the blatant hunger in his eyes. Deftly he dispensed with her bra and her own hands reached for the fastener at the top of her slacks. But Greg gave a brief shake of his head and placed her hands back at her sides. He undid the small silver clasp, then, placing his hands on either side of her hips, eased the white cotton slacks downward.

She stood before him almost naked, the silk bikini panties she wore beneath almost totally transparent. Her eyes were riveted on his face, watching as his eyes traveled the length of her. He stood then and swiftly picked her up. Renee, startled by the sudden movement, wrapped her arms around his neck for security. But he had no intention of letting her go, at least not until he had placed her in the center of the bed atop the soft comforter.

Then he backed away and Renee lay perfectly still as she watched him undress. She had seen him, of course, in the briefest of swimwear, yet she was shocked anew at the perfection of his body. Her eyes lowered slowly, taking in the muscled, precision-hewn body, followed the generous matting of soft brown chest hair as it narrowed in V-like form above his navel. Her heart felt as if it had jumped into her throat as she observed his taut, straining readiness for her.

With utmost restraint she lay still, watching with widened doelike eyes as he walked over to the bed and lay down beside her. The tingling sensation within her had by now expanded to a deep burning that centered within her loins, spreading in aching awareness throughout every inch of her body.

Absent completely were any thoughts other than what was happening here and now. Motives, consequences—none of that mattered. She wanted this man, wanted him with a primitive, instinctive yearning that was absolutely impossible to deny. But Greg was determined to satisfy that yearning at his own pace, slowly, methodically titillating her even further, driving her to the brink of fevered impatience.

He pulled her to him and kissed her deeply, thoroughly, but when she responded with equal ardor he withdrew, trailing his lips along the sides of her face. When he nibbled her earlobe, his warm moist breath tickling the labyrinthine contour of her ear, she squirmed in his arms and pressed tighter against him. Nudging her back somewhat, Greg raised up and poised his body over hers. Once more his lips lowered, traveling slowly downward, wetly tracing a pattern with his moist, exploring tongue. Methodically, expertly, he circled the deep pink aureole of each breast, flicking back and forth over each bursting bud with his tongue until an uncontrollable moan escaped her lips.

She was burning for him, all of him, but still he made her wait, pushing her further into a state of frenzied desire. His mouth moved lower, caressing her navel with feather-light kisses. Renee's hands were pressed against the back of his head, but when she sensed him moving even lower, her arms jerked upward in surprise and sudden anxiety. Greg looked up at her then and with a soundless movement of his lips reassured her, bid her to lay back down. And she did so, unable to resist the unbelievable sensation flooding her inner thighs as he slid her panties down her legs with caressing hands and then stroked her legs apart.

Renee was beyond attempting to inhibit the sounds coming from her. Pure sweet, rapturous ecstasy rippled throughout her loins as Greg's mouth and tongue probed further, driving her closer and closer to brink of total ecstasy. Her hands ground into his shoulders and suddenly he was pulling backward, moving upward to position himself over her. Her hands slid downward across his back and onto the smooth, taut flesh of his buttocks, pressing downward on them. When finally he entered her she was aching with readiness, aching to be one with this marvelous, passionate, loving man. Their bodies entwined at last. And as they rocked against each other, slowly at first, then with increasing rapidity, lightninglike seizures jolted through them both, the current of their passion reverberating along its arc, connecting them completely.

They lay curled up in each other's arms, the fire of their passion banked and spent for now. Renee's eyes were closed but she was far indeed from a state of sleep. Her brain was churning, trying desperately to make some sense of the whirlwind of emotions that had set loose a storm of after-the-fact effects she'd never thought possible, let alone even considered. God knows, she had never known such sweet, *complete* physical release in her entire life. That knowledge alone was riveting enough. But the experience had been more than just that; to term it as such would be nothing short of a fallacy. And she would not lie to herself about something as important as this. She couldn't. One did not unlearn something, especially something as valuable as this, she knew well enough that one basic fact of life.

And heaven above, she had learned something tonight with Greg that she hadn't even dreamed possible. She, who had considered herself worldly enough, experienced enough, satisfied enough. Imagine! Something inside flipped and rolled over and there came an instant quickening of her heartbeat. Fist to her mouth, she began to knaw on the knuckles of her fingers, filled with absolute wonder at this foreign, almost frightening emotion seizing her. Never had she felt so *close* to another human being, so part of something other than herself and what her own body was feeling. She would treasure the memory of this night in his arms forever. An impulse seized her; she longed to roll over, wrap her arms around Greg and bury herself next to him, just *be* there beside him. It was crazy! How could she feel like this after only having made love with him one time? And that one time would be the *only* time, an inner voice reminded her.

Slowly her eyelids opened and she stared straight ahead, seeing only shadowy outlines of the furniture next to the window. Her heartbeat slowed to a normal pace as the sobering realization hit her fully. So? This was exactly what she wanted, wasn't it? How well she had pulled it off. *Don't wish too hard for something you want; you might just get it.* Renee frowned and squeezed her eyes shut tightly. What a stupid, silly cliche, she thought with irritation, hoping like hell that she could manage at least a few minutes of sleep.

The jangle of the telephone awoke them the next morning. Greg picked it up, said "Thank you," then hung up. Turning onto his side—they had come apart sometime during the night—he tousled her tawny hair and kissed the top of her head.

"Time to get up, sleepyhead," he said.

Renee groaned and rolled over to face him. "What time is it?"

"Six thirty," Greg answered.

For once Renee was sleepy at this hour of the morning. Why couldn't she have felt this relaxed during the previous days of her vacation? As she reluctantly opened her eyes, her gaze fell upon the answer to her question. She hadn't been as relaxed, or even as remotely happy as now, simply because there hadn't ever been anyone like Greg Daniels in her life. She smiled warmly at him.

"What's that for?"

"What?"

"That smile. I don't think I've ever seen one like that on your pretty face."

"Pretty face, huh? I can just imagine." How different this was too, she reflected. For once she hadn't felt the urge to hurry out of bed and take a quick look in the mirror to make sure she was presentable for Louis when he awakened. How refreshing to know it didn't matter. And somehow she did know that. Greg's next words confirmed it.

He kissed her lightly on the forehead and whispered. "You *are* beautiful in the morning, Renee. Believe me."

She did. She believed he meant every word of it. "Do we have to get up?" she asked reluctantly.

Greg nodded. "Sorry. But we have to get you back to Oahu, remember?" Then he raised one eyebrow. "Unless, of course, you can think of a way to extend your stay."

Renee shook her head slowly. "That's impossible, I'm afraid. I promised the office I'd be back on Monday morning." And it was a promise she was sorely regretting by now.

"Well then, you'd better get your adorable bottom out of bed and get dressed. We have to check out of here in an hour."

With more reluctance than Renee had thought possible, she got out of the bed and gathered her things together to take with her into the bathroom. She switched on the hot water, then stepped into the tub for a quick shower. The feel of the pounding water on her skin elicited memories of other sensations her body had experienced last night. Suddenly the reluctance she'd felt earlier expanded to regret that she was leaving so soon. Today. With a pang she realized that the casual little fling she had executed so carefully had gone beyond the limited expectations of harmless pleasure she had counted on.

Then she reminded herself that whatever emotions she was experiencing at the moment were temporary anyway—certainly not worth getting overly concerned about. She'd had a good time with Greg, a damned good time. But like strangers in the night, they had merely fulfilled temporary vacancies in each other's lives. After a few short days of knowing each other, sharing each other so completely, he would go his way and she hers. Just exactly as she had planned.

CHAPTER FIVE

Renee cast one last glance at the small screen at the front of the cabin and yanked off the earphone set. She was tired of craning her neck over and around the seat in front of her; she had asked for a window seat not realizing she wouldn't have full view of the screen. Besides, it was a mushy, almost maudlin film, and she wasn't in the mood for heavy emotions right now. She wasn't in the mood for much of anything, as a matter of fact, except perhaps getting off this airplane, grabbing her luggage, and going home. But she really wasn't in the mood for that either.

"What's the matter with you?" Marcy whispered from the next seat. "Can't you keep still?"

"Sorry," Renee muttered, slumping down in her seat and crossing her arms over her chest.

"I thought you liked Redford."

"I do. But the movie's a little too dramatic for my taste."

Marcy cocked an eyebrow and studied her friend for a moment, then took off her own headset. "Hey, what's up, Renee? You look really down."

Renee shrugged and then opened her eyes. "I'm not down. I'm fine."

"Well, you don't look it. In fact"—Renee paused —"in fact, you haven't looked all right since we boarded the plane. Since we left Greg standing there staring after you with those *scrumptious* green eyes."

Renee rolled her eyes and shook her head slowly from side to side. "You do have a way of exaggerating, Marcy."

"Believe me, I'm not exaggerating when it comes to that." Her voice lowered dramatically. "My God, Renee, he's beautiful."

"You've said that about a hundred times since we got on this plane."

"And you've done nothing but clam up on me. Maybe if you'd answer some of my questions I'd shut up."

"All right." Renee gave in. "What is it you want to know?"

"About Greg. What you two did in Maui."

Reluctantly Renee began to relate the adventures she and Greg had shared yesterday, leaving out, of course, the more intimate details.

"Sounds like a dream," Marcy commented.

"It was fun," Renee admitted.

"When's he coming to see you?"

Renee glanced at her friend with a surprised expression. "He's not."

Marcy looked shocked. "He's not? But why?" Her eyes narrowed as she added, "He's not . . ."

"Married? No. He lives in Seattle and I live in Long Beach. We're not exactly neighbors." She refrained from mentioning that she'd given Greg her address and phone number when he'd asked for them. Not that she expected him to do anything with them however.

And it was just as well. Surely a man like Greg had lots of other women in his life. She couldn't imagine a reason in the world he could have to go to the trouble of contacting her once they were back on the mainland. He lived in another state, and she was already involved with someone else. The sobering knowledge that Louis wouldn't be back for another couple of months hung over her like a dead weight. But it was the truth and there wasn't a damned thing she could do but sit and wait for his return. Perhaps Marcy had been right all those times she'd accused her of being a fool for the man. That traitorous thought niggled at her and just how much of a fool she was was something she really didn't care to dwell on.

She and Marcy settled quickly into their normal routine at the duplex they shared. Each went her respective way during the day, usually meeting for dinner in the evenings and hardly seeing each other on the weekends. After only a week since their return, the trip to Hawaii seemed like years ago, and sometimes as though it had never even occurred.

Renee had slipped back into her job at the hospital almost as if she hadn't even left. But that had been relatively easy enough. Jobs of all types were in short supply these days, hospitals notwithstanding, and the personnel department was the first to feel the slack in workload, which was exactly the opposite of what Renee could have used at the moment. What she needed was a pile of work so pressing that she would have had to bring some of it home every night. Unfortunately there was barely enough to keep her going during the day and little to occupy her mind at night.

Marcy wasn't much help either. She worked as a buyer for a very successful chain of clothing boutiques. Though the two of them normally talked for a few minutes over dinner, Marcy usually *did* have work she brought home at night, which didn't help Renee's sense of loneliness at all.

She had eagerly gone through the mail as soon as she'd gotten back from Hawaii. The only correspondence she'd received from Louis, however, was another of his trite, hastily scribbled post cards. Always signed "love," of course, though Renee's initial pleasure at seeing that written indication of his affection was rapidly fading as more and more time passed and the long letter she awaited was not forthcoming. Naturally Louis always referred to the mountain of research he was involved in, and Renee could only assume that he probably *was* busy. Still, he could have found at least fifteen minutes somewhere to write her a more personal note than what he'd managed thus far.

At the same time, Renee realized she was being unrealistic, expecting something out of the man that he hadn't even been able to give her while he was here. He was simply not demonstrative as far as his emotions went. Nevertheless, the suspicion that she was making perhaps a few too many excuses for him continued to eat away at her.

More than tired of the repetitious pattern of thoughts, Renee walked into the kitchen and rummaged around in the pantry for something to prepare for dinner. She wasn't in the mood for cooking, especially after the phone call she'd received from Marcy when she'd gotten home. Would Renee mind getting out her suitcase and lending a hand packing a few of her things, she'd asked. She'd just made arrangements for a late-night flight to New York. An important buyers' meeting or something. Renee couldn't ever keep up with Marcy's hectic schedule. And the truth was, her roommate's busy schedule made her somewhat envious. Especially now.

Marcy had come home and, like a vicious whirlwind, showered, finished with the packing, then left. And now Renee was alone, trying to get up the necessary interest to prepare dinner for only herself. She stared absently at a box of rice, picked it up and looked at it disinterestedly, then put it back on the shelf. What was she going to do with it. Eat it raw? She sure wasn't in the mood to cook it or anything else. Sighing heavily, she shut the pantry door. Great time for a diet, she thought ironically.

She sauntered into the living room and plopped down on the sofa. What a drag of a Friday night. Reaching for the TV's remote control device, she studied it for a moment, then switched it on, leaving off the sound. A panty-hose commercial finished and the opening scenes of a rather dull sitcom came on. Renee tried to lip-read the screen, then, giving up, sat and watched dully for a moment. Suddenly her entire posture stiffened as another character appeared. Uncanny how his profile resembled . . . God, he looked so much . . . he looked so much like Greg! He could have been his twin. Unconsciously Renee's lips parted and she stared dumbly at the set.

What in the world was going on with her? Here she was, reacting to a television actor like some kind of idiot. But there was reason enough; so carefully had she shoved aside any thoughts about him in the week since she'd gotten back that this character who just happened to resemble Greg Daniels completely took her off guard. Renee punched the Off button on the remote control and watched the screen fade to darkness. She sat up straighter and placed an elbow on one knee, resting her chin against the knuckles of her hand. Nervously, she bounced the other leg up and down repeatedly.

This was absolutely ridiculous. She'd been bored to tears a few minutes ago, not even possessing the energy to prepare anything to eat. And now, though she was still not in the least hungry, she was a bundle of nervous energy—and all from turning on the stupid television set. She glanced down at her bare feet, then across the room at the new pair of jogging shoes next to the front door. Suddenly she jumped up. Now was as good a time as any to try them out.

She was already outfitted in running shorts and T-shirt, her usual around-the-house garb during the summer months. Quickly she slipped on a pair of socks and then the jogging shoes, tying the laces securely. Grabbing the housekeys, she remembered to switch out all the lights and make sure the doors were locked, then let herself out the back door.

As she was walking down the gravel driveway, she heard the telephone ring and almost stopped to go back inside to answer it. But by the time she got back inside, whoever was calling would have stopped, so she kept on going. The late June weather was warm, yet at this time of evening kissed with a sweet cool breeze. The sun wouldn't set for another hour and a half, Renee noticed, glancing at her watch. She was usually back within an hour anyway.

The new shoes felt good; light and springy as she set out on a course she had traced many times over the past year. She never tired of observing this charming neighborhood flanking the picturesque Ocean Boulevard. Everything was so colorful, the older, refurbished houses blending well with one another, perfectly manicured lawns a visual feast of lush shrubbery and pungent, well-nourished flowers.

Her footsteps quickened as her breathing became more adjusted to the steady, rapid pace. She was getting pretty good at this, she thought smugly. And to think she had been so out of shape only a year ago. Meeting Louis had certainly changed all that—she had to credit him with that much. Now, of course, there was a different motive behind her striving for physical fitness; she was doing it for herself, not for Louis's ideas of what constituted a perfect state of health and beauty.

By the time she reached the back door of the house, she was winded and damp with perspiration. The run had been exactly what she needed; her mind was clearer and she was in far better spirits than when she'd started out. She might even have enough energy to work out with the weights Louis had bought her for Christmas. How typical of Louis, she reflected wryly, to buy her such a completely unromantic, *practical* gift.

As she let herself in the back door the telephone was ringing again, so she hurried into the kitchen and picked it up on the fourth ring. "Hello?" she answered in a slightly breathless tone. She grabbed a handful of paper towels from the dispenser and wiped the back of her neck.

"Renee Michaelson, please."

"This is she." Renee's voice quavered slightly as she recognized the sound of his voice. But she was stunned by the extent of her reaction to it. How uncanny that he was calling now, after she'd seen his look-alike on television just an hour ago.

"It's me, Greg. Did I catch you at a bad time?"

"No . . . no, of course not. I just walked in the door."

"You sound out of breath."

"I was out jogging." She pulled the telephone cord out farther and took a seat on one of the barstools. "It's nice to hear from you, Greg. Where are you calling from?"

"Right now I'm in Seattle. Tomorrow, however, I'll be in L.A. As a matter of fact, that's why I called."

"Mmm-hmm," Renee replied teasingly. "And what particular purpose is that?"

"Well, little lady, I thought I might look you up while I was there."

"Is that so? Well, let me tell you something, Mr. Daniels, you'd better cut the 'little-lady' line or you ain't got a chance."

Greg chuckled. "Can't seem to help my chauvinistic impulses—they just sneak out sometimes. Well, anyway, how about it? Are you busy?"

"No. . . . What exactly did you have in mind?"

"Dinner, drinks, dancing, maybe a little fooling around . . ."

In spite of herself, Renee blushed as she almost giggled. "Greg Daniels! How dare you talk to a lady that way!"

"I thought you said you weren't a lady."

Renee clucked her tongue. "I said 'little-lady' not . . . Oh, what a ridiculous conversation!"

"I heartily agree. Besides, if I'm going to have any conversation with you at all, I'd sure as hell prefer it in person."

Renee laughed lightly. "All right then. What time will you be in L.A.?"

"Early. But I'll be tied up with business all day. I could drive out to Long Beach around seven."

"That sounds all right. Do you have a pencil handy? I'll give you directions."

After relating her directions, they chatted a few minutes longer before saying good-bye. Renee hung up the telephone and leaned back against the bar, stretching her legs in front of her, flexing her feet back and forth. Then suddenly she popped up and walked briskly to the pantry and opened the door.

"Nope, that's not what I want," she said aloud. Crossing the room to the refrigerator, she withdrew a can of beer. She popped the tab and tilted her head back and took a long swallow. Then, setting the can down on the counter, she let out a long sigh and smiled, immensely pleased with this positive change of mood.

Nothing like a good, long, invigorating run to clear one's head. No, nothing at all like it.

Friday was normally the fastest day in Renee's work week. Not this one. It seemed to drag on interminably and when five o'clock finally did arrive, she didn't waste a moment bidding her fellow employees good-bye and beating a hasty retreat down the hospital corridors to the parking garage. The traffic was every bit as tedious as the day had been, and she sighed repeatedly as she sat through one stop light after another.

Nervously, she tapped a forefinger on the steering wheel. What should she wear? If they went out to eat, which she assumed they would, it would depend on where they were going. The black silk pants with that new blouse would go well just about anywhere. Lord, what in the world was she doing getting as excited as some high school girl on a first date! This surely wasn't any first date, she reflected, flushing at the memories of that particular thought.

But she hadn't expected to hear from Greg, or at least she'd told herself she hadn't. Maybe the fact that she was so revved up over just seeing him again meant that she *had* expected to all along. One thing was certain; she'd been absolutely bored to tears lately and if this didn't pull her out of it, nothing would.

By the time she made it home it was twenty to six; there was still plenty of time to get ready. Relaxing somewhat, Renee spared a few minutes to slap together half a cheese sandwich, then sat down to watch a few minutes of the evening news while munching on it.

Afterward she straightened up the house, then drew a hot bath and laid out her clothes on the bed. Meticulously she went through her "getting-ready" ritual, the familiar actions themselves putting her in an easier frame of mind.

How long had it been since she'd gone to this much trouble getting dressed? A little over a month. Yet this time there was a distinct difference. She was dressing for herself this time, pleasing herself, not going to all this trouble for *him*—Louis. Somehow she was confident that it didn't matter a hill of beans what she wore. Greg would just as soon see her in a pair of cut-off jeans as the elegant after-five outfit she'd chosen.

Ah, yes, Louis . . . A meticulous dresser himself, he expected the same of her. Always. And if she didn't meet his standards, he didn't feel the least compunction in letting her know. Renee was brushing her hair when suddenly she tapped the handle of the brush against the palm of her hand. Strange, she mused. How long had it been since she'd had an affectionate thought about Louis? She couldn't really remember. Ever since he'd left she'd been filled with resentment, and now that she thought of it, not all of it caused by his leaving her. Little things about him, idiosyncrasies that she'd chosen to ignore in the past, kept creeping up in her thoughts like this. Matters that were now, from a quite different perspective, rather irritating.

Oh, she was so just so damned confused, she didn't know what she really thought about the whole relationship. If only he wouldn't have gone, she wouldn't be having all these insecurities. And doubts . . .

But on the other hand, she smiled inwardly, there was one positive aspect of Louis's absence. She had met Greg. Strange, how much she had missed him this past week. Missed him? The intrusive thought brought her thinking up sharply. Had she really missed him? Was that why she was behaving so excitedly, simply because of his coming tonight? Such contemplation only succeeded in raising more questions than she was prepared to answer at the moment and as she lifted the brush once more to run it through her hair, she determinedly shoved aside any further thoughts in that direction.

The doorbell rang at seven thirty-five. As Renee placed her hand on the knob she felt her heartbeat quickening. Her anticipation, she soon discovered, was certainly appropriate. She had almost forgotten the startling effect of Greg's incredible good looks. And there he stood on her front porch, all six feet three inches of him, dressed in a pair of charcoal gray suit pants, pale blue shirt, striped tie loosened at the neck, and jacket slung across one shoulder. He was looking in another direction as she opened the door, affording Renee a momentary unobserved appraisal. And it was a good thing; she needed the second or two he took to turn to her in which to compose herself. But when she met the startling grass-green gaze, she swallowed spasmodically.

"Hi," he said with a slow, sexy smile. Renee noticed for the first time faint shadows beneath his eyes, and the grooves along his mouth were somewhat deeper than she remembered.

She returned the smile, pulled back the door even wider, and said, "You made it."

Greg entered the living room, then stood in the middle of it as she closed the door. "Did you think I wouldn't?"

Renee laughed. "Well, you never know. Getting out of L.A. can take an entire lifetime. Especially the time of day you started out."

Greg's gaze quickly swept the room, then came back to study the woman before him. Her soft brown hair was brushed out to a radiant fullness and her dark-brown eyes shimmered. The black silk pants flowed loosely yet hugged her long, lean legs with the slightest movement. The spaghetti-strapped white satin camisole draped smoothly, daringly, over her firm high breasts.

Something stirred deep within Renee as Greg's gaze moved over her and as she walked toward the kitchen she said brightly, "Sit down, I'll be right back."

In the kitchen she picked up the tray she had prepared earlier; two glasses and a bottle of white wine and a platter of cheese and crackers. She dallied for a few moments in the pantry, searching for napkins she'd forgotten to include on the tray. Why should she be feeling timid like this?

Lord knows, she had been intimate enough with Greg. Was that what was bothering her? That perhaps she'd made a mistake in falling into bed with him almost as soon as they'd met?

But that was completely irrelevant. She hadn't cared at the time what he might think, so why should she start now? She was nervous just because she hadn't expected to even see him again. *So shut up and get back out there,* a tiny, impatient voice urged her.

"Here," she said, setting everything down on the coffee table. "I thought you might be hungry by the time you got here. And thirsty."

"Ah, perfect." Greg smiled at her and accepted a glass of wine. "You look beautiful."

Renee laughed dismissively and smiled back at him. "Why, thank you, Mr. Daniels. You don't look half-bad yourself." She eyed his loosened necktie and said, "Maybe a little tired?"

"Yeah," Greg said on a sigh, "it's been one hell of a day, that's for sure."

"When do you have to go back?"

"Whenever I'm finished. Tuesday at the earliest." Greg closed his eyes and leaned his head back, running a hand through his hair.

Renee gave him a thoughtful look, "You know, Greg, I'd assumed you were going to take me out to dinner."

His eyes popped back open and he answered hastily, "I was. Are you hungry?"

Renee smiled. "Actually I'm starved." At Greg's sudden move forward, she raised one hand and said, "But I've got a better idea."

"What's that?"

"Well, it's obvious that you are absolutely bushed. Why don't I just run down to the market, pick up a couple of steaks, and make something here?"

Greg's expression indicated relief, but he said carefully, "That's ridiculous. You're all dressed up and . . ."

"And you're no more in the mood to go out than the man in the moon."

Greg smiled sheepishly. "Do I look that bad?"

"You do look tired." Renee stood up and said determinedly, "too tired to go anywhere. So. No more questions. Here." She moved to switch on the stereo, setting the volume low, then returned to where Greg now sat straight up, elbows on his knees, watching her with undisguised hunger.

Ignoring her warning, she pushed on his shoulder until his back rested against the couch. "Now you get comfortable while I—"

Suddenly he was grasping her hands, pulling her down until her face was mere inches from his and she was almost off-balance.

"Greg!"

"Shhh . . . you talk too much, woman."

He brushed his lips against hers, plying them open with undisguised impatience. But Renee needed no further persuasion and she invited the welcoming warmth of his tongue, met it with her own in equal probing fervor. She lost her balance then and suddenly landed in his lap. A rush of memories so pure, so sweet with rapturous promise invaded her senses and she wrapped her arms around his neck, her thumbs massaging the tense muscles along his nape.

Her mind whirled with the import of what she was doing. What was she doing? The man had only moments before walked through her front door, and look at her now, all over him! Suddenly she pulled away from him, her face and neck flushed with pure physical reaction—and obvious embarrassment.

"Greg," she said rather shakily, "do you want me to or not?"

"You know I want you to," he muttered thickly.

Renee smirked. "You know what I mean. Do you want me to go to the store or not?"

"You want the truth?"

"Of course."

With a sigh, Greg said, "I'd give my eye teeth not to have to get back in that car for a few hours. Yes, I'd love for you to feed me."

"Then let me up." Renee squirmed and reluctantly Greg released her.

Renee went into the bedroom to fetch her purse, grateful for the opportunity to compose herself a little. By the time she walked back into the living room again, Greg was slouched down, head back and eyes closed. For a moment she thought he was asleep, but at the jangle of her car keys he opened his eyes and smiled at her.

"Anything in particular you'd like?" Renee asked.

With a languid smile, Greg replied, "Surprise me."

"All right. I will. See you in a little while."

The dinner Renee prepared—with a little help from Greg, who had by now revived a bit with the wine and cheese—turned out to be at least as good as anything they might have ordered in a restaurant. They talked easily while they cooked and ate, about their work, their friends, all sorts of things. And when they were finished Greg helped clean off the table while Renee loaded the dishwasher.

"You're really different, you know that," Renee

commented, watching from the corner of her eye as Greg scraped and stacked the dishes on the counter then whipped open the refrigerator door and placed the butter and the salad bowl, neatly covered with plastic wrap, inside.

"What's that supposed to mean?"

"You're rather domestic for a male member of the species. It's rare, in case you haven't noticed," she grinned.

Greg accepted the wrung-out dish cloth Renee handed him and began to wipe off the dining room table. "I guess it comes from years of living alone. And good training from a mom who didn't believe in the menfolk getting away without doing their share of the household chores," he added.

"Hooray for your mom," Renee proclaimed enthusiastically. "The world could use a few more of her type."

"I take it that's the type of mom you're going to be?"

Renee slanted a glance at Greg and smiled wryly. "I don't remember saying anything about mothering being in my plans for the future."

"No . . . you didn't. But is that what you would like? Someday?"

Renee shrugged and thought about an appropriate answer, unaware that she was rinsing the same dish over and over again instead of placing it in the dishwasher. "I suppose it's a possibility," she answered evasively.

Greg leaned back against the counter and folded his arms across his chest, his green eyes studying her closely—too closely. "Then that must mean you have marriage included in your future plans, too."

Renee gave a forced laugh. The conversation was taking a decidedly much too personal turn. "Well I certainly don't believe in producing a child out of wedlock." She slid the plate into the dishwasher and said brightly, "And what about you, Mr. Daniels? What are your plans for marriage? And kids, of course."

Greg's answer was prompt and easy. "Oh, I want them both."

Renee struggled to hide the surprise she felt at his answer; wasn't this the one subject most men were reluctant, if not downright churlish about discussing? After all these months of wanting to discuss nothing else, how odd, how completely hilarious, that it was *she* who felt decidedly uncomfortable with the subject. She brought the dishwasher door up, switched it on, then turned around and dried her hands briskly on a towel. "Come on, let's get out of here. This thing makes a terrible racket."

Renee brought two glasses and the rest of the wine into the living room and turned on the television. The subject of marriage and children had been conveniently discarded—at least for now. The movie they watched was reasonably interesting and entertaining, but that was the least enjoyable perspective of the evening. Greg was just such a wonderfully easy person to be with; indeed he had proven himself to be so in every setting they'd shared thus far. Renee had become so completely relaxed with him that as the hour became later it seemed only natural for Renee to extend the offer for him to stay. "I just thought since you would have so far to drive back to L.A. and all . . ."

"Believe me, you couldn't have had a better idea," Greg said, picking up her hand and stroking small circles across her palm with the tip of his index finger. "In fact, Miss Michaelson, I like the idea immensely." Reaching up with his other hand, his thumb circled the pulse point at the base of her throat. "When did you say your roommate was coming back?"

"Not until next Friday . . . or Saturday." Renee could sense her breathing becoming slower, shallower.

"Perfect. Just . . . perfect." And he smiled a big sexy smile that made her want nothing more than to melt into the warm, sweet comfort of his arms.

CHAPTER SIX

Renee was astounded anew by the depth of response Greg's lips upon her own elicited. How marvelous this felt—so right, so good, so perfect. She was drawn to this man like none other, even Louis. Why did she have to be hung up on Louis? Why couldn't Louis have been like Greg, warm and generous and fun to be with? Why couldn't Greg have come into her life before him?

The questions whirled round in her head in a frustrating argument. It was far more pleasant to set aside the troublesome thoughts and enjoy what was happening here and now. Renee remained on Greg's lap as they kissed, until he leaned slightly against her, pushing backward until she was in a half-lying position.

"My God, Renee, do you know how much I've missed you this past week? It seemed like a year."

His voice was low and husky, his breath against her ear sparking a thrill that left her quivering.

His hand trailed slowly along the column of her neck, his palm resting for a moment upon her collarbone before moving farther down to cup her breast. Then with his hand flattened, almost arcing backward, he gingerly moved it in slow sensuous circles, the friction of fabric against her bare breast hardening its peak to a stiff, aching bud.

Renee closed her eyes and sucked in her breath, instinctively arching her body upward. She raised one arm to wrap around his neck but it stopped in mid-air; suddenly the air was pierced by a strange high-pitched whine, immediately followed by a rapid, noisy clattering sound.

Greg jerked backward and Renee's eyes flew open, her gaze locking with his in total bewilderment.

"What in hell . . . ?" Greg muttered.

The clattering sounded again, followed by the same whine. Renee's eyes lit up in sudden recognition and she sat up straight as the rattling sounded again.

"Oh, my God, I don't believe it." Renee's mouth widened into a grin.

Greg moved to allow her room to stand up, but he asked dryly, "Are you expecting someone? Dracula maybe?"

Renee giggled and popped up off the couch. "Not Dracula, but someone with pretty similar bad habits."

Greg looked perplexed and somewhat annoyed as he watched her bound out of the room, then finally decided to follow her. Whatever or whoever was making all the racket was obviously somewhere at the rear of the house and he came up behind Renee just as she opened the door to the back porch.

A streak of brown and orange and white flashed past her and Greg quickly flattened himself against the wall. Seeing him, Renee burst out laughing, but quickly trotted past him to the kitchen.

Her squeals of delight mobilized him and as he cautiously glanced through the kitchen doorway, he saw her squatting down on the floor, her face and hands buried in the abundant fur of a calico cat.

"Peter Murphy, where have you been this time?" Renee cried. "Taking care of all your pretty girl friends? Took your sweet time, didn't you? I was beginning to get worried."

Renee cooed to the cat in a sing-song voice and as she stood up to face Greg, she turned the cat around, holding him just below his front legs, the back ones dangling down around her stomach. "Peter Murphy, this is Greg Daniels. Greg, this is Peter Murphy."

Greg rolled his tongue around the inside of one cheek and said, "Uh-huh." He raised a hand in a limp wave and said, "Glad to meet you, Peter—what the hell kind of name is that? Peter Murphy?"

Renee frowned in mock offense and turned brusquely as she walked to the refrigerator. "The name is Peter Murphy. And there's nothing the hell wrong with it. It's a very decent name." She rummaged around in the refrigerator and withdrew a can of condensed milk and a small, foil-wrapped can.

Setting the cat back down, she pulled a couple of dishes out of the cupboard. "Here you go, P.M., I saved you some of the seafood delight."

Greg rolled his eyes and leaned back against the counter, watching Renee's ministerings to the sleek tomcat.

"You didn't tell me you had a cat," he said.

"You never asked."

"True. How long have you had him?"

"Since he was a kitten. He's a big boy now, and he's not always inclined to stick around. He disappears now and then, sometimes for a day or two, sometimes up to four or five days in a row. This time was the longest. He left last Sunday and I was starting to get worried. I guess he got hungry."

Greg laughed. "No kidding. He's lapping that up like he hasn't had a meal all week."

"But he looks fat, doesn't he? He doesn't look like he's been suffering any, does he?" Renee sounded genuinely concerned and Greg said, "He looks like he's probably had more than he could handle if you ask me. Maybe one of his girl friends gave him a hard time."

Renee grinned at that. "Yeah. Is that what happened, Peter Murphy? Did you get into trouble?" She slid down onto the floor, crossed her legs, and watched the cat greedily devour what she had given him. She began to massage the scruff of his neck and for all intents and purposes appeared to have forgotten about Greg.

"Renee?"

"Mmm-mm?"

"Uh, are you just going to sit there?"

Renee looked up at him innocently. "I'm sorry, Greg. It's just that I haven't seen him in . . ."

Greg held up one hand. "That's fine. Go ahead

with your reunion. You don't happen to have a beer, do you?"

"Sure. In the frig. Help yourself."

Greg took a beer from the refrigerator, popped the tab, and took a swig. He watched Renee for a moment, amazed at this new side of her personality. With a wry smile he shook his head from side to side slowly. "If you treat your kids anywhere near the way you're doting on that cat . . ." he muttered.

Renee glanced up at him and frowned. "What? Finish what you were going to say."

Greg took another pull on the beer and raised both eyebrows as his gaze went from the cat to Renee. "You'll raise a bunch of brats, that's what."

Renee's mouth parted and she clutched the tomcat close to her bosom, her chin raised defiantly. "Oh yeah? Well, you can keep your opinions to yourself, Greg Daniels."

Can of beer in one hand, Greg waved the other as he turned and started out of the room. "Don't worry, I won't offer any more. I'll be in the living room."

"All right. I'll be there in a little bit."

Greg rubbed the back of his neck and cast Peter Murphy one last derisive glance as he went on into the living room. Opinion or not, the romantic mood was pretty much dispelled, for the moment anyway.

A "little bit" turned into a full quarter of an hour as Renee devoted herself to making sure the tomcat had enough to eat and filled his catbox with fresh litter. Peter Murphy seemed to take all the attention for granted and was soon curled up in his favorite corner of the kitchen, purring loudly with contentment.

"Want another beer?" Renee called out to Greg from the kitchen.

"No, I'm fine."

Something about his tone seemed different, cooler, and for a moment Renee thought perhaps she was imagining it. But when she added, "I'll be right there," and Greg didn't respond, a small frown etched her brow.

She walked into the living room and saw that he was slouched down comfortably on the couch, leafing through a magazine.

"Want to turn the TV back on?" she asked brightly.

But Greg merely puckered his lips and kept on turning the pages. He was obviously ignoring her. Then as Renee sat down opposite him on the love seat she noticed the thick brown photo album lying next to him. A stab of anxiety shot through her and she licked her lips nervously. She moved forward, attempting to reach for it, when Greg abruptly put the magazine down on the coffee table and picked up the large leather album.

"Nice album you have here," he commented, running his thumb along the edge of it.

Renee muttered a small, insignificant sound, then said, "Wh-where did you get that?"

Greg lifted one shoulder and nodded in the direction of the lamp table. "It was laying right there. You don't mind my having a look at it, do you?" He looked directly at her then, and Renee flinched beneath the hard glint in his eyes.

"No, of course not. Why should I?"

"That's right. Why should you?"

But Renee cringed as he opened the heavy binder to the first page of plastic-covered photographs.

"Pretty good shots. Who took them?"

"Umm. I don't know. Marcy took some of them. I forget." Suddenly she shot out of the chair and reached across the coffee table to grab the album. "Look, they're really not that interesting. I—"

But Greg's hold on the book was firm and he easily pulled it out of her grasp. "Oh, I think they're interesting enough." He turned the page and let his gaze roam slowly over the next two.

Renee flushed deeply. Why hadn't she remembered to put the damn thing in the closet instead of leaving it out? But she had forgotten about it completely. And certainly she'd never expected Greg to show any interest in it. But anyway she had no reason to feel so defensive—it was none of his business. But as Greg's gaze perused each page she wanted to shrink into the floor. She knew the pictures he was looking at by heart. Pictures of her and Louis—lots of them, in various locations and poses. The two of them on the beach, here in the house, outside on the lawn, skiing in Lake Tahoe. Intimate pictures with intimate poses, none of which she had any desire to share with another man.

"Who is he?" Greg asked in an off-handed tone.

"Who?"

He cast her a derisive look and said, "The guy in the picture. The one you're hanging all over."

Renee hesitated. She'd already told him she wasn't

involved with anyone. She couldn't . . . "Just someone I used to date."

"*Used* to?"

"Yes." Renee's voice rose somewhat. "What's the big deal?"

"You're not seeing him anymore?"

Renee's answer was quick, almost too quick. "No! I'm not."

Greg flipped back to the first page. "Looks like the two of you were pretty heavily involved."

Renee's face tightened and she flushed with anger. "I really don't care for this inquisition, Greg. I haven't asked you a damn thing about who you've dated. I don't even know if you're seeing someone else right now." Suddenly her heart was pounding heavily in her chest. "Are you?"

Greg's answer was slow in coming, but his gaze held such intensity that she flinched beneath it. "I'm surprised you would even ask that."

Renee frowned. "What kind of answer is that?"

Suddenly Greg reached forward and grasped her hands, pulling her down beside him. "I wouldn't think you'd even need an answer. I would think you'd know it already."

"Why?" Renee asked in a little voice.

"Because it's obvious, that's why." Greg smiled gently. "What do you think I'm doing here?"

"Well, you had business and—"

"And I just happened to work you into my schedule?"

Renee shrugged and bit her lower lip. "Yeah, something like that."

"Well, you're wrong." He cupped her chin in his

palm and tilted her head, forcing her gaze to meet his. "Did you think I could make love to you in Hawaii and that would be the end of it? Just a short little vacation rendezvous?"

Renee swallowed deeply and the pounding of her heart increased as something else took hold—genuine fear. She didn't want to hear him say any of this. It was wrong. For both of them.

"My God, Renee," he said, his voice thick with emotion. "I'm in love with you. I think I have been from the moment I saw you there on the beach."

Suddenly she wanted to cry. He'd said it. Said what she couldn't bear to hear. Oh, Lord, how in the world was she going to handle this now? "Please don't say this, Greg," she whispered, looking away.

"Why not? It's the truth. I love you. And if you don't love me . . . yet . . . that's okay. I can wait."

Renee looked back at him in surprise. "Greg. I—I don't know what to say."

"You don't have to say anything. Just tell me what the guy in those photographs means to you. Because if there's something important going on here, I want to know. Now."

Renee looked down at her hands and bit down on her lower lip so painfully she thought it might bleed. But she didn't care about that. Oh, what was she going to say! Why was it so hard for her to tell him the truth? She had already lied to him once by telling him she wasn't involved with anyone. What was happening to her? Was she turning into a pathological liar? No, she couldn't accept that sort of self-incrimination. She was just confused. Confused about her own feelings toward both men in her life. Admittedly, she certainly hadn't felt this doubtful about her feelings toward Louis until after she'd met Greg. Angry, resentful, yes, but not this unsure of herself. The fact of the matter was she didn't know where she stood, what she wanted, except for one thing. One very important thing. She knew she wasn't ready—she just couldn't give Greg up . . . not yet.

Slowly she shook her head. "I can't tell you that he *never* meant something," she conceded in a small voice. "He did."

"Are you still seeing him?"

Renee shook her head. That *was* the truth. At least for now. "No. I'm not seeing him."

Greg's hands squeezed the flesh of her upper arms and he smiled at her. "Then that's all I need to know."

Renee glanced up at him, her brown eyes widened in fear. Greg laughed softly and said, "Don't look so worried, babe. It's all right. What are you so afraid of?"

She shrugged and chewed on her upper lip now. "It's . . . I—I just wasn't expecting this kind of conversation, that's all."

"Actually"—Greg lowered his head to hers, his lips grazing her lightly furrowed brow—"I'm kind of tired of talking myself." Sliding his hands upward, he cupped the sides of her face as he kissed her on the mouth thoroughly, deeply.

Renee felt her posture slowly slipping backward as Greg pushed against her, lowering her to the couch, covering her chest with his torso. As they continued kissing, Greg adeptly slid the spaghetti straps of her top to the side, then reached beneath her to unfasten the buttons at the back. When she lay bared to the waist, his gaze simmered at the sight of her firm, full breasts. Then he lowered his head, taking one roseate crest between his lips, his tongue wetly teasing the stiffened buds. Renee groaned and sunk her teeth gently into his taut, corded neck. Greg's hands had found the zipper of her slacks and within moments the silken material was gliding down and over her hips and legs, her panties, hooked in the crook of his thumb, along with them.

Renee fumbled with the buttons of his shirt, then turned onto her side to allow him room to lay beside her. She heard the plop of his shoes on the carpet and the slick sound of his leather belt being removed. As Renee undid the last button of his shirt, Greg shed himself of both it and his pants. He turned then, his full, naked length wedged snugly against hers. An involuntary shiver coursed through Renee as their bodies pressed against each other, their legs and arms and hands intertwining, roaming, exploring, reuniting.

The familiar burning began to build within Renee as Greg lifted her slightly, burying his head in the soft valley between her breasts. She heard him moan and her need quickened, propelling her into an initiation of her own. Moving until her body was above his, she arched her back, revelling in the teasing agony of Greg's tongue as it flicked around and against each swollen nipple. His hands traveled the length of her back, cupping then gripping her buttocks. When she thought she could stand no more she lowered her body to his completely, moaning aloud as he slid within her.

She looked down at him, her hair falling in a shimmery brown curtain on both sides of her face. She could see the barely restrained control in his flushed features, and as his hands grasped her hips she saw in his eyes that he wanted her to be still. Resting her chest against his, her body became limp as Greg's strong hands rose and moved her hips up and down, round and round. The fire within her leapt to raging proportions, and when she heard his deep, shuddering groan beneath her, her own explosion erupted, washing over her in wave after wave of warm, sweet sensation.

Renee's eyes fluttered open. She was growing cold, but Greg's breathing was deep and regular and she hated to wake him. But, despite the soothing comfort of his limbs entwined with hers, she was becoming uncomfortable. With difficulty she attempted to extricate herself, and when she finally managed to, Greg awoke. He mumbled something unintelligible and closed his eyes, easing off into sleep once more. Renee smiled and snatched up her clothes on the floor, then tiptoed across the room and down the hall to the bathroom.

She showered quickly then donned the terry-cloth robe that hung on a peg on the door. She read the wall clock as she walked back into the living room; it was almost one A.M. Quickly she switched off the light above the dining room table, then returned to stare at Greg, totally relaxed in sleep on the sofa. He looked so absolutely peaceful that way. On impulse she went to the hall closet and withdrew a pillow and blanket.

Lifting Greg's head, she slipped the pillow beneath, then threw the blanket across him. He didn't move and she stood there for a moment, watching, listening to the steady rhythm of his breathing. A lock of his hair had fallen across his brow and she reached out to pull it back then stopped herself.

An unfamiliar sensation swept over her just then; she found she could not move, let alone pull her eyes away from him. How strange, this powerful pull she felt toward him, an emotion that went far beyond the sexual attraction they shared.

His words of earlier, before their lovemaking, came back to her then and she shivered inwardly. *Was* it true? Did he really love her? A tiny voice piped up, *what would Louis think about that?*

Who cares what Louis would think, Renee answered back angrily, then frowned at the unwonted sentiment. She'd spent weeks caring about just that; what Louis would think of just about everything she had done. But Louis's opinion was insignificant. What *was* significant was the man lying before her—a man who had told her tonight that he loved her. The very words that Louis doled out with such stingy infrequency.

But as much as she'd always longed to hear them, Renee had always realized how easy they really were to say. What really mattered was the man himself, his actions, his beliefs, his character. And of all the men she'd ever known, Renee knew, with a conviction so positive it was absolute, she had never even *met* a man with the strength of character Greg Daniels possessed. How easy it would have been for him to have simply taken advantage of her in Hawaii—as she had done with him, she reflected with an embarrassed twinge—to have used her for nothing more than a casual vacation fling. But he hadn't. He'd called her soon after they were back, just as he'd said he would. That very trustworthiness alone put him far beyond Louis. Greg was a caring person, sensitive to *her* needs, as well as his own. How often had she felt that way about Louis? Hardly ever, Renee reflected grimly. But most of all she simply loved *being* with Greg, loved having him around, loved the sound of his voice, the teasing sparkle in those fantastic green eyes, the way his body merged with her own, teaching her in such a short time the *real* meaning of that elusive term "lovemaking." He slept so soundly, so securely on her couch, as if he belonged there. Renee experienced a quick stabbing sensation in the pit of her stomach as she suddenly pictured her life *without* him. How could she, after knowing him this well, even stand it?

There was a message in here somewhere, a very strong, convincing one. The question was whether Renee had the strength to listen to and consider it. She clenched one hand and rubbed her knuckles against her chin. Slowly, she turned and walked from the room. Sleep would come with great difficulty tonight, there was no doubt of that. Her brain, her heart, were churning with a thousand conflicting emotions and doubts. She could only wonder what it would take to come to terms with it all.

CHAPTER SEVEN

Marcy's buying trip to New York couldn't have been better timed, Renee quickly decided. What had previously promised to be a most boring weekend alone turned out to be one of the most enjoyable, satisfying periods of her life. Greg's business, which kept him in L.A. until the following Tuesday, fortunately did not take up any of the weekend. After Friday night his staying with Renee for the duration of his trip was simply assumed.

The weather, which was ideal so much of the year in this part of California, did not disappoint them. The sunshine beckoned and after breakfast Saturday morning Greg pulled his jogging suit—which he always brought along on business trips—out of his suitcase. The two of them started out, Renee setting the course for a four-mile jog that took them through her neighborhood, then into the nearby village of Napoli, a rich stretch of quaint ocean-front cottages, each with its own yacht dock. Sea gulls squawked and the sea breeze cooled them as their footsteps hit the pavement in synchronous pacing, Greg shortening his longer stride to match Renee's. Afterward, back at the house, they cooked together, took care of the household chores, and made love that night until both were completely and delightfully exhausted.

On Sunday Renee pulled hers and Marcy's bicycles from the garage and she and Greg went on a fifteen-mile ride. They were exhausted by the time they got back to the house and took a delicious, refreshing afternoon nap, then later enjoyed a seafood dinner at a bay-front restaurant. By Monday Renee's enthusiasm for her work had returned in full strength, no doubt due in part, she admitted, to the fact that Greg would be there when she got home. Although she often enjoyed the solitude Marcy's absences provided her, she wasn't really a loner, and much preferred having someone to come home to.

And Greg was far more than that, of course. In the space of a few days he had made himself a part of her life, had become her friend, her lover, a man for whom she had utmost respect and admiration. That her feelings for this wonderful man were rapidly overshadowing the love she felt—or thought she still felt—for Louis was a mental burden that became harder and harder to bear. She should, of course, simply make up her mind about what she was going to do with the situation and take it from there. It was the logical, fair thing to do, yet something didn't add up, some resolution had not yet been attained, either emotionally or rationally. She wasn't able to put her finger on it, but she sensed that the reason had to do with the fact that she needed to see Louis in order to work this whole thing through completely. And, too, despite Greg's claim that he was in love with her, she simply found it hard to believe, given the amount of time they'd known each other. She needed time, time to know him better. Time to know for certain her own needs and desires.

Despite those heartfelt sentiments, however, she was achingly aware on Tuesday morning that her feelings for Greg had progressed further than she could have ever expected. His leaving just after breakfast brought back all the feelings of abandonment that Louis had provoked—only this time it was worse. Now confusion compounded the situation. At least then there had been only one man complicating her life, one set of feelings to deal with.

As she sat at her desk Tuesday afternoon her thoughts were far removed from the file folder that lay open before her. Louis's image kept floating before her mind's eye, only to be overshadowed and then replaced by Greg's. He had promised he would be in touch soon, yet he had not specified when he would call and already she was wondering if he would. Which was absolutely ridiculous. The man had said he loved her, wanted to be with her, and they had enjoyed such a marvelous time while he was here. But now that he was gone it was hard to believe she had spent four days with him, made love the way that they had. Louis had hardly entered her thoughts at all.

It was ridiculous the way her mind kept chasing the same thoughts round and round. She was getting heartily sick of it! She thought about going home that evening to an empty house and the prospect filled her with nothing but dread. But that's the way it would be if she and Greg were married. He traveled so much, surely there would be times when she'd be . . . What was she doing, thinking of marriage to Greg! Especially after she had spent the last year dreaming of being the wife of Dr. Louis Mandol, had set her entire life around pursuing that one goal. That was just it—marriage to Louis had been her goal, but Louis had not seemed interested in even trying to meet her halfway.

What does that tell you, Renee? a small voice piped up. That perhaps the affair with Louis *was* a one-sided situation after all—as much as she'd tried to deny it, to Marcy and to herself over and over again. It was hard to admit it, there was no doubt of that, and in Renee's case, pride had held its ground quite well in keeping the nasty truth from her conscious mind.

And now, little by little, she was coming face-to-face with the reality of the situation. She couldn't make Louis love her, couldn't make him marry her. She wasn't even so sure that was what she wanted anymore either. There was Greg to think about now, for it was he who had stirred all these realistic sentiments to the surface. Much as she would have liked to ignore the whole thing, there were serious issues at stake here and she needed to come to grips with all of them, most of all what it was she *really* wanted.

By Friday she was sick of her own company and at the back of her thoughts all day long was the fact of Marcy's return that evening. Despite knowing she'd probably end up listening to one of her friend's frequently espoused lectures, she was in sore need of her company—and a good, reliable sounding board.

Greg had called yesterday, sounding exhausted yet happy that he'd reached her. He wasn't sure what his schedule would be like for the next week or so, but he'd get back to her as soon as possible. He wanted to see her again—soon—and Renee had agreed that she missed him too. She really did.

Marcy was frazzled and peaked-looking from the hectic week she'd spent in New York. The cross-country flight had just about worn her out and Renee was afraid her "talk" would have to wait another day. But as soon as she uncorked a bottle of wine and put supper on the table—she'd prepared Marcy's favorite chicken dish—Marcy was wide-awake and ready to hear what had happened while she was away. She wasn't disappointed in what she heard. Renee's involvement with Greg had apparently been deeper than she'd suspected, and she was obviously pleased to see her friend so confused.

"How can you say that, Marcy? I'm about out of my mind by now!"

Marcy cocked one eyebrow and grinned conspiratorialy. "Now, I wonder why is that?"

"You know very well what I'm talking about," Renee threw back. She swallowed another healthy portion of the wine and went on. "I'm not supposed to be involved with someone else. Not like this anyway."

"Why not? Last I heard you weren't a married woman."

"Don't be sarcastic."

Marcy threw out one hand. "Who's being sarcastic? I was merely pointing out a fact." She leaned forward over the table, her elbows resting on the edge. "I've told you a million times and I'll tell you again, you owe nothing to Louis Mandol. You put far greater stock in the relationship than it deserves."

That stung. Renee replied sharply, "That wasn't necessary, Marcy Lindstrom. I was in love with Louis and you—"

"Was?" Marcy looked smugly amused.

"Am . . . whatever. Oh, what difference does it make?" Her voice trailed off vaguely.

"Go on," Marcy prompted.

Renee sighed and finished the glass of wine, then refilled it. "God, Marcy, I'm so confused. I don't know what to do."

Marcy sat back and crossed her arms over her chest. "All right, look. Let's just take it real simple, okay?"

Renee hesitated, then nodded.

"How long has Louis been gone?"

"A month and a half."

"And how long have you known Greg?"

"Less than three weeks."

"But you've spent a lot of time together, right?"

Renee nodded.

"Enough for Greg to think he's in love with you, right?" Renee nodded and Marcy asked, "Do you feel you know him very well?"

Renee raised both eyebrows and nodded slowly. "It's funny, but I feel like I've known him for at least as long as Louis."

"And after one year of knowing Louis you were

still surprised when he pulled that trip to Zurich without asking you along. Doesn't that tell you something?"

Renee sighed heavily. "I suppose it does." She looked up at her friend with widened, innocent eyes. "Then why can't I accept it? Why can't I just blow the whole thing off like you've told me to so often?"

Marcy smiled affectionately. "Because you're too faithful, that's why. You hang on until the very last. I guess that's what makes you such a good friend too."

Renee sighed and looked down into her glass. "I haven't been very faithful since Louis has been gone."

"And you admitted yourself he probably wasn't either."

Renee laughed wryly. "That's for sure."

Marcy sighed this time and she studied her friend thoughtfully. "I don't know what else to tell you then, Renee. You know all the facts. They speak for themselves. Only you can decide what you're gonna do about them."

"Yeah," Renee answered softly. "I suppose you're right." She looked up and smiled self-deprecatingly. "I'm gonna have to be more like you and learn how to get my act together."

Marcy chuckled and shoved a hand through her hair. "Ha! You wouldn't think that about me if you'd been with me this week."

"What happened?"

The conversation moved into a discussion of the problems and frustrations Marcy had experienced on her buying trip to New York, and for the next hour and a half Renee found comfort in thinking about someone else's problems. By the time she crawled into bed she had firmly decided to put her quandary on hold for a while and she quickly settled into a sorely needed relaxing sleep.

Greg called Saturday morning. He was in Dallas and would be back in Seattle on Monday. He would call her then. Perhaps she'd like to make plans for the next weekend? Renee said yes, she definitely would. Just hearing his voice, even if he was halfway across the country, warmed her, made her feel as though he were here in the house with her again. She was astounded once more by the depth of emotion the man provoked in her and when she hung up could only hope that the weekend would fly by until she could talk to him on Monday.

It did. The instant she walked into the house that evening the telephone was ringing. Quickly she let herself in, flung her purse on the kitchen counter, and snatched up the receiver.

"Hello?"

"Hi, honey. Did you just get home from work?"

Renee smiled at the sound of his voice. "Just walked in the door. How was Dallas?"

"Hot as hell. But successful."

"Great," Renee enthused. "Who did you snare this time?"

Greg hesitated. "You don't really want to hear the details, do you?"

"That's not fair," Renee chuckled lightly. "I think your work is exciting." She paused. "But actually I'd rather know what you've got up your sleeve for next weekend."

"How does L.A. sound?"

"Fine. But perhaps we could stay somewhere . . ." Renee's voice trailed off uncertainly.

"Your roommate's back?"

"Mmm-mm."

"Well, I'll be in L.A. only for a couple of days anyway, so it would be better if you could meet me there."

"All right then. Where will you be staying?"

Greg informed her of where she should meet him and they talked for a few minutes longer. Sometime, he said, when things slowed down a bit for him, he wanted her to fly up to Seattle. Renee said the idea suited her just fine, and she hoped his work slowed down real soon.

She hung up in a cheerful frame of mind, since they had made definite plans, yet she wished the week would fly by the way the weekend had. It was a shame to be wishing so much of her life away like this. She should be enjoying every moment of it. When was she going to slow down and live for the moment? Resignedly, she supposed whenever she could make up her mind exactly what it was she wanted in life and with whom she wanted to share it. Unfortunately, she was still hampered from making that decision. Especially after what she discovered in the mailbox when she got home the following Thursday evening.

Addressed in the familiar scrawl, on a pale-blue air mail envelope—surprise! not the routine post card—was Louis's handwriting. For a moment she just stared at it, unable to think what to even do with it. There was a time, and not too far in the past, when she would have ripped it open before she reached the house. Now she merely held it in her hand and walked slowly back to the house, aware of a strange mood creeping over her—a presentiment perhaps?

Well, what does he say? one small voice wanted to know. *Who cares?* another answered. One thing was certain: The only way to answer either question was to read the thing.

Marcy wasn't home yet, so she put fresh coffee and water into the automatic coffee maker and sat down at the dining-room table with a letter opener. Gently she slid the stainless-steel blade through the delicate paper and lifted out the single sheet. She unfolded it carefully and began to read. The task was accomplished quickly, for it was a short letter and, as usual, Louis was to the point. He would be home two weeks early and would she still be able to pick him up at the airport?

Not a word about how much he missed her, how glad he would be to see her, only that he needed her for something. But then, as she'd reflected before, Louis wasn't the sentimental type, and to expect him to be so in a letter was a touch unrealistic. Nevertheless, Renee reread the letter, searching for messages between the lines. Resignedly, she admitted there were none.

So. He would be home in less than a month. How odd, this lack of caring one way or the other. But in a way she was glad to feel this way. She was sick of the emotional upheaval the man had always elicited within her. Perhaps she was getting over that phase of the relationship. And if that were the case, then what phase was the relationship in now?

The question became an issue later that evening when Marcy found the letter still lying on top of the table where Renee had left it. Neither had been really hungry and Renee had popped a bowlful of popcorn, which the two of them were now munching on. The letter had been lying on the edge of the table and had almost fallen off when Marcy pushed it back. She frowned at the unfamiliar-looking envelope and asked, "Hey Renee, what's this?"

"What?" Renee was at the refrigerator, filling their glasses with Coke. Holding a glass in each hand, she bumped the refrigerator door shut with her bare foot and walked back to the breakfast nook. Then she recognized what Marcy was referring to and a shadow fell across her features.

"This letter," Marcy said, holding it up. "Is it from who I think it's from?"

Renee pulled out her chair and slumped down in it, reaching for a handful of popcorn. "Yep."

Marcy regarded her friend for a moment, then said, "You don't look too excited about it."

Renee muttered something unintelligible, shrugged, and continued to chew.

Both were quiet for a while, then Marcy asked, "Are you still going to L.A. this weekend?"

"Sure. Why?"

"Even after the letter?"

Renee frowned. "What does the letter have to do with it?"

"Nothing from my point of view. I just thought you might think just the opposite."

Renee cast her friend a direct look. "Okay, Marcy, what are you getting at?"

"We've covered this subject before," Marcy said in a warning tone.

Renee waved a hand. "Might as well cover it again. Just say whatever you have to say."

"First of all, I'm curious to know what Louis wrote."

Renee turned the corners of her mouth down and reached for a single kernel of popcorn. "Nothing much. He'll be here a couple of weeks early and wanted to know if I'd still pick him up at the airport."

"That's it?"

"Yes."

Marcy snorted. "That guy's about as romantic as warts on a bullfrog."

Renee rolled her eyes ceilingward and sighed. "I can't change the man, Marcy. What do you want me to do?"

"Give up on the jerk!" Marcy suddenly exploded. Renee stared at her in surprise. "You've got a perfectly nice guy," Marcy went on angrily, "hell, a real knockout, telling you how much he loves you, and you're still hanging on to that bore."

"He's not a bore, and I resent that." Embarrassingly, she could hear the lack of conviction in her voice.

"You do, eh?"

Renee refused to answer. She had let Marcy get started on this, and now she was regretting the impulse.

"I just don't see how you can juggle two guys at

once the way you're doing. What are you going to do when Louis is back?"

"I haven't figured that out yet," Renee said in a low voice. She was staring at the kernel she still held in the palm of her hand, as if wondering how it had gotten there.

"All right, all right," Marcy said in a more subdued tone. "I know you're getting sick and tired of hearing me expound on this, but just remember I'm doing it for your own good."

Renee looked at her with a pleading expression and Marcy relented. "Okay, I'll shut up. Want to watch television while we finish the rest of this?"

"Yeah, sure."

The conversation hit a sore spot, however, and once again Renee was plagued with considerations of what all was involved in continuing to postpone what needed to be dealt with now. Late at night, as she lay wide-awake in bed, she was forced to admit that indeed her feelings for Louis were not the same. Even if they were judged by the effects of one letter, she knew it to be so. Nevertheless, she wouldn't know with absolute certainty what those feelings were until she saw him in person and had it out with him about their relationship face-to-face. Of course, she had tried that tactic before and Louis had always responded the same—delaying an answer concerning his intentions, but keeping her hanging on by the emotional hold he'd always maintained over her.

Expectedly, her weekend with Greg was tainted by Louis's letter. Despite her enthusiasm over the time they shared together and the sheer happiness and fun over simply being with Greg again, the letter was always there in the back of her mind, the knowledge that in just a few weeks she would be picking him up at the airport and they would be together again, just like before.

But that wasn't true, was it? Nothing was just like before. It probably wouldn't have been even if Greg were not in her life. In her life and in her heart. And he was. Very much so. And she didn't want him out of it either. The trip to L.A. confirmed that beyond her strongest doubts.

Yet despite the marvelous time they spent together, which consisted mainly of staying in the luxurious hotel room Greg had booked, lounging around watching television, eating in bed, and making love with total abandon, Renee held back some tiny portion of herself. It was impossible for her not to. At the back of her mind was the constant question of how she'd feel when she did see Louis again. And she couldn't help wondering how he'd feel if and when she broke the news to *him.* But about a matter far more significant than a temporary separation.

Her concentration level was so abysmally low, in fact, that she hardly gave notice to Greg's statement that he would be coming back to L.A. in a few weeks. A mistake, she discovered soon enough, that she would sorely regret.

CHAPTER EIGHT

Though they were unable to see each other for the next week and a half, Greg telephoned faithfully. Renee had written back to Louis saying that yes, she would pick him up at the airport, and each and every day the event weighed heavily on her mind. Indeed the truth of the matter was she was almost dreading it.

She thought over and over about what she would say to him, what he would say to her, and for the life of her could come up with nothing. Marcy wisely didn't broach the subject again, but her opinions on the matter had been voiced often enough. Increasingly, those opinions hit a sensitive chord within Renee.

The bottom-line question remained unchanged: did she or did she not still love Louis? Lately, she kept answering with another question: had she ever loved him to begin with? Or was it just an illusion she was in love with, a mere image of what she had believed was important to her happiness, her future.

But, more importantly, how did her relationship with Greg fit in? It was undeniable now that what had been intended as a neat opportunity to even the score with Louis had backfired. She was more deeply involved with Greg than she ever could have imagined. Incredibly, the man claimed he was in love with her. And she believed him. But what were her true feelings? Could it be that she was falling in love with him too, perhaps already was in love?

The questions were agonizing yet certainly she couldn't ignore them much longer. As a juggler, she just didn't rate, that was for sure. Her nerves were already frayed from rehashing the situation over and over again. In a way she was grateful that Louis had decided to come home early. She didn't think she could stand too much more of this indecision.

The flashing message on the overhead computer terminal indicated that the Pan Am flight had just arrived. Renee stood in the middle of the crowded waiting area, watching the arrival door as passengers began to walk through. She'd arrived at the airport only a few minutes earlier, frazzled from the hectic drive and rattled even more trying to find a parking space. She was out of breath from the half-walk, half-jog down the unending corridors and now, as her gaze scanned the deplaning passengers, her shoulders were taut, her expression indicating anything but joy.

She saw him. First his sandy-brown hair bobbing along the corridor, then his face as the passenger in front of him moved out of the way. Briefcase in hand, tie in place, he looked relaxed and confident, exhibiting none of the signs of fatigue one would have expected from the seven-thousand-mile trip.

As usual, he was impeccably dressed, his clothes only slightly wrinkled from the strain of travel. He looked around, his expression expectant, but Renee restrained herself from waving to him. Let him see her first. What would he do, she wondered, if she weren't there as she'd promised? She watched his expression harden a little in irritation, then she stepped out from behind the post that had obscured her from his line of vision. He saw her then and instantly his face relaxed as he walked toward her.

"Hi," Renee greeted him, remembering to smile. Strange how little she felt. Unbidden, a cool, confident reserve had replaced the nervousness she had been ineffectively struggling against these past weeks.

"You made it on time," Louis commented as he sat his briefcase down on the floor and reached inside his inner jacket pocket for his luggage claim tickets.

Typical, Renee observed. No "Hi, honey, I really missed you," no "Hello," even. How had she put up with that for so long?

"I almost didn't though. The traffic was horrendous."

Louis smiled then and lowered his head to kiss the crown of her head. "You look good. How have things been?"

Renee didn't kiss him back, instead gave a dutiful smile and said, "Thanks. Nothing much happening at work actually. We've even had several layoffs lately. Mostly within the nursing staff."

"Hmmm. The recession's really hitting everyone these days."

They were walking along toward the baggage claim now, and as they conversed, Renee couldn't help reflecting how easy it was. She felt as if she were talking to an old friend she had agreed to pick up at the airport. Good lord, was that what he had become? An old friend?

By the time they'd left the terminal and reached the car, Louis was waxing on about the unexpected wealth of research contacts he'd made in Zurich. He talked and talked, his tone imparting the savior-of-the-world attitude that Renee had been so awed by at one time. Now, as she listened with feigned interest, nodding and making the appropriate responses to what he was saying, she was aware of a growing disdain for Louis's superior attitude. Certainly he was involved in a very important field—cancer research—and was making a tremendous contribution to society. Very impressive, but she was sick of being impressed by Louis. In fact, she couldn't give a hill of beans for what he did anymore. Was that what had constituted her attraction for him, made her dance like a puppet every time he pulled the strings? How ridiculous, but worse, such a waste of her time.

She said hardly anything, merely produced a plastic expression of interest while Louis rambled on, her brain whirling with thoughts and reasons and motives for her involvement with this man. She was shocked by the resentment and anger welling up within her, much of it directed at herself for having been fool enough to hang on for so long.

Thankfully, they were soon in Long Beach and she was driving along the street to Louis's ocean-front penthouse. She pulled up in front of the multistoried building and Louis stopped his endless expounding on his Zurich exploits long enough to turn to her with a rather surprised expression. "Aren't you going to park in the garage?"

Renee frowned. "No. Why?"

The surprise deepened. "Do you have to be somewhere? I thought you would want to come on up."

"Oh," Renee said, understanding what he was getting at. "Umm . . . actually, I promised Marcy I would be back before eight. Her car has been giving her trouble and I promised her she could use mine." As good a lie as any. She smiled and said with exaggerated consideration, "I'm sure you must be exhausted anyway."

"Well, I am rather bushed," Louis admitted on a sigh. He opened the car door, pushed down the seatback, and began to remove his luggage from the back seat. When it was all settled on the concrete drive next to him, he leaned back into the car, stretching across the console, cupped his fingers around Renee's chin, and planted his lips on hers. He kissed her languidly, expertly, benevolently.

Promptly he pulled away and bestowed one of his best smiles on her. "I'll see you tomorrow." He winked and withdrew from the car.

Renee smiled blandly and as soon as he had spoken with the doorman, who had just stepped up behind him, she drove off. She drove automatically back to her house, hardly conscious of anything other than the strange surge of emotion welling up inside. She just couldn't believe Louis was the same man. He looked the same—perfectly groomed, crisply efficient in that faintly superior demeanor she knew so well. He sounded the same, his medium-pitched, professional tone going on and on as it usually did about his favorite subjects—himself and what he was doing. He even kissed the same—and she had felt absolutely nothing.

He was exactly the same as he had been when he left, only now she was responding to him in a completely different, totally unemotional, manner. The change had been within her. The realization of this undeniable fact suddenly struck her full force. Her reaction to it, however, was somewhat surprising. She felt lightheaded, almost giddy with the sense of freedom. God, she didn't need this jerk! She couldn't stand him! *Marcy, oh, Marcy, wait till I tell you how right you were.* Then she remembered; Marcy wouldn't be home until Monday. She had gone out of town for the weekend with a business associate.

Oh, well, it didn't matter. She could tell her as soon as she saw her. By then, of course, Dr. Louis Mandol would know of her decision also. She had no intention of continuing their relationship on any level. She almost snickered as she imagined his pompous reaction. Breaking up would no doubt seem more his category than hers. But, then, maybe he wouldn't even care. What the hell! It didn't matter anyway. She didn't care how he responded. All she cared about was this tremendous feeling of release—release from the mental turmoil that had been dragging her down for the past few months. For the past year actually.

Greg's face loomed before her and she felt an exquisite ache for him. She missed him so much—light-years more than she had thought she missed Louis. He'd said he would be in L.A. on business again soon, hadn't he? She hoped so. If not, she'd simply make an airline reservation and hop on a plane to Seattle and see him.

It was Thursday night; she usually heard from him on Friday night if not on Thursday. Hopefully he would be in on Saturday. She couldn't wait to see him.

She was a little late leaving the hospital Friday because of a budget conference that had dragged on most of the afternoon. By the time she parked the car and let herself into her house, the day's heat was subsiding a bit. She wasn't really in the mood for a run, though it would probably do her some good. She changed into her jogging shorts and a T-shirt and was about to prepare a light supper when a familiar scratching sounded at the back door. Grinning to herself, she opened it, and Peter Murphy slunk inside, rubbing up against one of her legs and then the other before strutting into the kitchen for his chow.

"What have you been up to, P.M.?" Renee asked. She forgot about her own dinner while she set about filling one of the tomcat's bowls with milk and the other with half a can of cat food. She watched him dig in, completely ignoring her presence in lieu of one of his favorite passions—eating. Whatever he did do during the day certainly burned up the calories, Renee reflected.

She was in the middle of cleaning some lettuce for a salad when she heard tires rolling on the driveway outside. She frowned, wondering who it could be, when the front doorbell rang.

"Be there in a sec," she called out, but it rang again a couple of more times. "Just a minute," she yelled with a touch of irritation. "Goodness," she muttered to herself as she nearly tripped over a bag of cat litter she had picked up on her way home but had forgotten to put away.

She peeped out the keyhole before unlatching the locks and suddenly her whole body became tense. It was Louis. She was still holding the bag of litter and shifted it beneath one arm as she pulled back the door. "Hi," she greeted him, not bothering to smile.

Louis was dressed in his most casual style—designer jeans and a starched western shirt, with dark-brown leather boots. "Thought you'd be home by now," he said, entering the house. Suddenly he focused on the package she was holding. "What is that?"

"Kitty litter," Renee said, shutting the door behind him.

Louis wrinkled his nose in distaste. "You still have that ugly creature?" he asked, only half-teasing. Renee knew only too well of his dislike of her cat, of pets, period. She had once excused that particular trait of his to his occupation; he worked on an almost daily basis with animals, experimental ones, and as a result saw them from a different perspective than most people. Now, however, she felt only annoyance at his remark, which in light of her obvious affection for Peter Murphy was downright rude.

"I don't consider him ugly in the least," she said, turning her back and walking into the kitchen. Why hadn't he called to let her know he was coming? She wasn't in the mood to see him and, furthermore, she had already decided that she was going to have it out with him when she did. The only aspect she was looking forward to in doing so, however, was in getting it over with.

She was bent over, trying to fit the bag of litter into a very full kitchen cupboard. Louis walked into the kitchen and helped himself to a beer in the refrigerator.

"Hurry up and get dressed so that we can go for dinner."

Renee hesitated, then continued rearranging the contents of the cupboard. "You wanted to take me out for dinner?"

She heard him swallow, then set the can of beer on the counter. "You haven't eaten yet, have you?"

"No," she answered, standing up and slapping her hands together briskly. "I was just getting ready for a run."

She turned to him just in time to see his gaze run lazily down the length of her body. When he lifted his eyes to hers she noticed a hungry spark within the brown depths. Rather embarrassed, she turned and stooped down to stroke P.M., who was nudging up against her.

"You've obviously been doing a lot to keep in shape," he commented. Wow! Such a compliment; she should have it framed.

"Yeah, I have." Suddenly everything was reversed. The standard she had once measured other men by was now held in sharp contrast with another. Every single act, every word the man uttered registered in her brain against what Greg would have said in a similar situation. And Louis Mandol was left wanting—extremely wanting.

"It can wait, can't it? The run?" The suggestion sounded more like an order, and as Renee glanced up at him, her dark-brown eyes glinted stubbornly.

"Actually it can't. If I wait too much longer it'll be dark, and I don't run after the sun has gone down."

Louis looked mildly surprised at her tone and as he picked up the beer and drained the rest of it, he regarded her coolly. "Is something bothering you, Renee?"

Renee shrugged. "Well, for starters you could have called and let me know you were coming."

Louis looked really surprised at that. "Oh? I'd have thought you'd be glad to see me."

Renee said nothing and Louis prompted, "Well?" He laughed in that superior tone of his. "Aren't you glad to see me?"

Renee gave P.M. a last hug and rose, crossing her arms over her chest as she leaned back against the countertop. "About as glad as you are to see me, I suppose."

Louis frowned. "What's with all the word games, Renee?" He took a few steps to stand just in front of her and placed his hands on her shoulders. His frown deepened as he felt her tense. But he obviously thought he knew the solution to that as he bent his head, lowering his mouth to hers.

Renee turned her head sharply. He pulled back to

study her curiously. "Now, what is it, Renee? What's bothering you?"

Renee slanted her gaze to meet his and answered sarcastically, "Funny how you're so concerned about the way I'm feeling *now.*"

Louis rolled his eyes and sighed. "Oh, God, not that again."

"Not what again, Louis?"

"The fact that I didn't want you to come with me to Zurich." He let go with one hand and circled the inner collar of his shirt with his forefinger. "God, Renee, when are you going to get it through your head that it just wouldn't have worked out? Our being there together?"

"Why not?" Renee threw back at him. "Because it would have inhibited your freedom while you were there?"

Louis's expression darkened and he said, "Okay. What are you getting at?"

"You know damn well what I'm getting at." She paused, and now that he had released his hold on her shoulders she crossed her arms again. "Tell me something, Louis." Her mouth tilted into a wry grin. "Did you see anyone while you were there?"

He looked at her blankly for a moment, then said, "Why do you need to ask something like that, Renee?"

"Simple. I want to know."

Louis shrugged. "All right then. I saw lots of people when I was there. It was impossible not to when —"

"Women," Renee clarified, though she knew

damn well he knew what she was talking about. "Did you go out with other women?"

Louis's gaze leveled on hers and his mouth grew taut.

"Why do you want to start this?"

"Why not finish it?" Renee's eyes sparked with an odd enthusiasm. "Did you?"

He hesitated for a long while, then spurted out, "Yes. As a matter of fact I did. Now. Does that satisfy you?"

Renee pursed her lips and nodded slowly. Incredible. The very information she had dwelt on, had agonized over all these weeks, didn't mean beans! It didn't hurt at all, hearing him confirm her suspicions. In one simple admission he had set her free and God, she actually loved it! Loved hearing him say what he'd just admitted.

"Mmm-hmm," she answered, suddenly wanting to laugh. "It satisfies me real well." She paused for a moment, then said in a clear, calm tone, "Get out of here, Louis." In just the same tone she would have used in saying, "I'm going to the store. Be back in a minute."

Louis looked as if he hadn't heard her correctly. He uttered a half-laugh and moved toward her.

Niftily, Renee ducked away and walked into the living room. Louis followed behind, obviously confused, and as she placed her hand on the doorknob of the front door, he said, "Come on, Renee, stop being so dramatic."

Renee raised her eyebrows. "I'm not being dramatic. I meant what I said, Louis. Get out."

Louis ran a hand through his hair and shook his head.

"Do you see what I mean? What good did it do for you to ask me that question?" He moved toward her and stopped, seeming to struggle for the right thing to say. Which was undoubtedly a highly unfamiliar situation to him. "She meant nothing, Renee. Really. You were here, I was there." He spread one hand palm outward. "What did you expect? I was gone almost three months."

"What I expected is exactly what you did," Renee stated coldly. "I can't believe how stupid I was to hang on so long. I should have told you it was finished between us before you left."

Louis smiled and said, "You're angry, Renee. That's understandable. But don't say things you're going to regret later."

Renee looked at him in utter fascination. "You know . . . you're absolutely incredible. The *only* thing I regret is that I let this stupid relationship last as long as it did."

But nothing she said appeared to faze him, for Louis's face still held the same condescending expression. Suddenly he closed the distance between them and grasped her by the shoulders, pulling her roughly against his chest.

Renee gasped. "What do you think you're doing?" she hissed.

Louis merely ignored her and, turning on his most sultry gaze, lowered his head, pressing his lips firmly against hers, his tongue attempting to force her lips apart. Renee protested with a moan, for that was all the sound she could get out. Louis's hand was on the back of her head and he held her securely in his grasp. Infuriated, Renee struggled against him, crying out against the pain of his teeth against her closed lips.

He slid his other hand, which had lain against the small of her back, beneath and up her thin T-shirt, pressing his palm against her breast. Renee jerked furiously and he pulled away long enough to utter "Just relax, damn it. Quit acting like a bitch" before he forced his lips on hers again.

Incensed, Renee was ready to haul off and let him have it where he wouldn't forget. She was just about to bring her knee straight up when the doorbell rang three times in succession. *Saved by the bell,* she thought hilariously. Louis eased back and asked gruffly, "Who the hell is that?"

"God damn it, let me go!" Renee spoke in a raspy voice. She didn't care who it was, at least she had been spared any further mauling by this beast. What an ass he was! Ignoring her disheveled appearance, she walked hastily to the front door and opened it. She almost gasped again. It was Greg, standing on her porch, looking unbelievably cool and handsome and eager to see her.

"Greg! You didn't . . ."

"I know. I called twice, sweetheart, but I guess you weren't home. I was so eager to get here I decided to just drive on over in the rental car." He entered the living room and came to an abrupt halt upon seeing another man standing in the middle of it, glaring daggers at him.

Louis jerked his chin upward pointedly and said, "Who is this?"

Renee swallowed deeply, her brown eyes widened to enormous proportions as they swung from one man to the other.

"I suppose I could ask the same," Greg said slowly, turning his gaze from the stranger to Renee. In doing so, Renee saw his expression alter, as if he were seeing her clearly for the first time. His gaze moved slowly down her body, taking in the mussed hair, her flushed cheeks, and the burnished, almost bruised appearance of her lips. Her blouse was lifted higher on one side than the other and she looked genuinely frightened—or guilty.

Louis's lips were of an especially bright color and his hair too was mussed from its otherwise perfect coiffure. Greg's eyes narrowed somewhat as he confronted Renee. "Have I interrupted something, Renee?"

Flustered, Renee said too quickly, "Of course not. Louis was just leaving."

"Is that so?" Greg commented.

"Greg, this isn't what it looks like," Renee said with a note of desperation in her voice.

Louis snorted. "Isn't that the truth. I guess it is a little hard to tell what's real around here." He shoved his hands inside his pockets and withdrew his car keys. "Who's been seeing someone else while we were apart, Renee? I can't believe I listened to all your self-righteous crap." He strode quickly across the room and was out the front door by the time Renee turned to face Greg. But any relief over Louis's leaving was quickly dampened by the look on Greg's face.

His normally open features were granite hard, and

with a sinking sensation in the pit of her stomach Renee knew she had already lost before she could even present her case.

Greg didn't even say anything, just moved toward the front door himself.

"Greg, wait," Renee said, stepping in front of him. "Please, let me explain."

"What's to explain?" Greg's green gaze burned with sudden knowledge and pain. "That's him. The guy in the pictures. The one you're not supposed to be involved with." His voice dripped sarcasm.

"I'm *not* involved with him! I'm not involved with anyone. Except you . . ." Renee's voice trailed off. She hoped that was still true.

Greg said nothing, but it was obvious he didn't believe a word of her protest. "I . . . I *was* involved with him," she admitted feebly.

"Since I've known you?"

Renee looked down at the floor sheepishly. "Yes. But he was gone."

"Where?"

"He was in Europe."

"I see." Suddenly comprehension flooded his features. "Oh, I get the picture. While he was there I was just someone to fill in the gap. How convenient."

"No! You weren't that." But guilt was written all over her face and she heard it in her voice herself. "I mean, I didn't mean . . ."

"You didn't mean to use me," Greg completed for her.

Renee was agonized and she reached out to Greg. "Greg, let me . . ." But he stepped around her and withdrew his own set of car keys. "Forget it. Don't bother to explain. I'm not entirely stupid."

Without a backward glance he let himself out the door and was in the car backing out the driveway as Renee stood helplessly at the door, watching him leave.

CHAPTER NINE

Renee stood rooted to the same spot just inside the front door, unable to move. She was in shock; it was as if what had just happened had been a dream, a nightmare. Yet it had happened, and unbelievably in just the space of little over an hour. Her first instinct had been to jump in her own car and race after Greg, but he was gone before she had time to get her wits together. And, anyway, she had no idea where he was staying in L.A. or how long he'd be there. She could call every hotel in the area, but that would take hours and no doubt would prove fruitless.

She felt something against her bare leg and finally she looked down. It was Peter Murphy. He looked up at her, his almond-shaped green eyes seeming to ask what she was doing standing there for so long. Like most cats, Peter Murphy's affection was doled out on his own time, and like most cat owners, Renee took what she could get. She bent down and scooped up the cat in her arms, then went to sit in a wing chair near the front window.

Peter Murphy purred contentedly as Renee rubbed him down in all his favorite places—under his chin, the scruff of his neck, and along his spine. Renee stared straight ahead as she automatically stroked the cat, who had no inkling of how long she sat or how she really felt. She was sick beyond expression over what had just occurred. The only thing that met with her approval was the fact that Louis had finally gone. She felt sure he would leave her alone from now on. But Greg. Oh, God, why hadn't he just stayed and listened to what she had to say? She could have explained everything.

But what could she do about it now? He was obviously furious with her for what she had done; lying to him about something he had insisted on clearing up from the beginning. How stupid could she have been? Holding on to the image of her relationship with Louis, thinking she had to give him another chance—for what? To prove his love for her? She hadn't even really loved him, and look what she had discovered anyway.

If she'd only been straight from the beginning with Greg. She could have explained the whole situation to him, and he probably would have gone on seeing her anyway.

He might have even helped her see everything in a more realistic light. But no, she'd been far too stubborn to let someone else's opinion influence her. Look how hard Marcy had tried to convince her that she was wasting her time with Louis. She'd had to learn that lesson for herself and in the process had paid for it heavily.

Peter Murphy raised his head for a second and gave it a quick toss. The droplet that had landed on his nose was a mere prelude to the steady flow that began to course down Renee's cheeks. Her heart ached heavily; her head pounded. Had she really lost Greg for good? "Damn," she whispered. "Damn, damn, damn."

She was crying steadily now and in the process had ceased her stroking of the cat. Peter Murphy cast her one disdainful glance, then, deciding she wasn't going to continue, hopped off her lap and sauntered out of the living room. Renee was far from noticing anything other than the regret and sorrow that gripped her. Gradually the tears subsided, and after deciding that the backs of her hands weren't enough to wipe away the dampness of her face, she got up and went into the bathroom. She took one look at her swollen face and bent over the sink, turned on the taps, and began to splash cold water all over her face and neck. Burying her face in a big clean fluffy towel, she felt a little better and walked into her bedroom and stood by the window.

Twilight was quickly fading into a night sky; in a few minutes it would be completely dark. There was no way she could run now. And she needed the exercise now more than ever, Renee reflected wryly. What other way was there to deal with this turmoil and unhappiness inside? And naturally Marcy wasn't here when she most needed her.

Well, Renee thought, plopping down on the edge of her bed, *I'll have to deal with this one by myself.*

At least for now. She lowered herself slowly to a reclining position and stared up at the orange glow the bedside lamp cast on the ceiling. She just had to get herself together, decide what she was going to do about this mess. First she had to decide what she wanted. That was simple. She wanted Greg. More than anything in the world, she wanted him. She had to get him back. She couldn't worry about the chance that he might not want to come back. Somehow she just couldn't see how his love for her could dissolve so quickly. If nothing else, she deserved a chance to prove to him that she hadn't meant to hurt him. She was just ignorant and confused. Ignorant enough to believe she was in love with Louis when she was in love with Greg.

A thrill coursed through her at the unexpected admission. She did love him. God, she loved him so much she wanted to shout it at the top of her lungs. She wanted him to hear it loud and clear. Suddenly she shot straight up and agitatedly ran her hands through her hair. She had to do something. Anything to get in touch with him. She had to talk to him, beg him . . . anything to get him back.

She stood up and walked around the room for a moment, trying to decide what approach to take. She didn't know where he was staying in L.A., or even if he still was there. He might even be on his way back to Seattle. Opening the top drawer of the night stand, she withdrew her personal telephone directory. He'd given her his address and phone number, though she had never used it before.

Her fingers shook as she dialed the long-distance number and she had to redial twice. "Come on," she muttered between her teeth, finally getting it right. It didn't occur to her that it was impossible for him to be home already.

Sitting down on the edge of the bed, she twisted the cord between her thumb and forefinger as she waited for the ringing on the other end. It rang twice and when a click sounded she drew in a sharp expectant breath. His voice, a recording, came on the line and she swallowed spasmodically at the mere sound of it.

"Hello, this is Greg Daniels. I'm away from the telephone at the moment, but if you'll leave your name and number, the time and day you are calling, I'll get back to you as soon as possible. Wait for the beeping sound before you speak."

Crisp, cool, and efficient. She'd never heard his business tone; given the circumstances, she felt intimidated by it. Indeed, she was so uptight that she began before the beeping noise and hung up in frustration. She drew in a deep breath, trying to calm herself before she dialed again. She lifted the receiver and began to dial slowly and carefully, and by the time Greg's voice had delivered its message she was ready for the sound of the beep.

Embarrassed, she cleared her throat, then said, "Greg, this is Renee. Please give me a call when you get back. Believe me, there is so much I need to explain. Please call . . . it's very important." She hung up. Well, she'd done it. Now all she had to do was wait and hope and pray that he'd be kind enough to do as she requested. But it was going to be hell until he got back to her. If he ever did.

* * *

By Monday morning Renee was a complete nervous wreck. Greg still hadn't called and she had phoned back several times, hoping he would be home and answer. But all she kept hearing was the stupid recording, which by now she was thoroughly sick of. She left two more messages but was scared stiff over the prospect that he would be angry enough to ignore all five of them.

When Marcy walked in the door Monday evening, having just gotten in from her long weekend, Renee practically jumped on her. She was eager to share with her friend this agonizing torment.

"I thought you would be back early today," she said accusingly. "Don't you have work to catch up on?"

Marcy cocked an eyebrow at her friend as she let her suitcases plop to the floor in the middle of the kitchen. "What's with the third degree, kiddo?" Placing her hands on the small of her back, she bent backward and stretched. "God, that feels good. Seems like I was born on that damn Santa Monica freeway."

"Did you have a good time?" Renee's question was rhetorical, her tone perfunctory.

Marcy looked at her curiously for a moment, then sauntered over to the refrigerator to pull out a can of Coke. "Great, as a matter of fact." She popped the tab off and sat down at the table, stretching her jean-clad legs out in front of her. "Why do I get the impression you don't really give a darn whether I had a good time or not?"

Renee was still wearing the dress she'd worn to work; she'd been in too agitated a frame of mind to remember to take it off. She stood with her back against the bar and twisted the smoky topaz ring on her left hand. Her eyes had dark circles beneath them, and as she looked over at her friend, Marcy noticed the obvious pain within them.

The can made a small clunk as she set it down on the table. "Hey, what's wrong, Renee? You look as though you saw a ghost. Or a whole roomful."

"Nothing that easy to handle," Renee muttered glumly.

"What is it? What happened?"

Marcy listened quietly while Renee told her everything that had happened while she had been out of town. When Renee was finished she drank the rest of her Coke and threw the can into the trash. "Well, you've definitely got a problem with Greg, but the part about Louis is the best news I've heard in ages. You finally came to your senses."

Renee waved a hand in the air dismissively. "Oh, Marcy I couldn't care less about that. I want to know what to do about Greg. I'm going crazy."

"What was he so upset about when he left?"

"I told you. I lied to him. He asked me not just once, but twice, if I was involved with someone else, and now he knows I was—even though I really wasn't. Oh, hell, he knows I was using him, and he'll never forgive me."

"You don't know that," Marcy countered. "He said he loved you, didn't he?"

Renee nodded.

"Well, if he really does, he's not going to let you go that easily. His pride's been injured and that's a tough one to get over. Especially for a man."

"Well, what am I gonna do?" Renee practically whined.

"Calm down, first of all. Come on, let's go into the living room and we can discuss your strategy."

As they made themselves comfortable in the living room, Marcy stretched out on the couch, Renee on the love seat. Renee finally began to relax. Marcy always helped put things in perspective so well, made things appear so workable. And after an hour's worth of discussion, Renee began to think that there really might be hope.

Renee's first objective, they both agreed, was to get Greg's attention. Until she had that she could do nothing but sit and twiddle her thumbs—or bite her nails to the quick. If he hadn't answered her call by Wednesday, then she would have to resort to more drastic methods. Like what, Renee had wanted to know.

"Leave a message that something dire has happened, or is going to happen, if he doesn't call you."

Renee stared at her friend thoughtfully. "I've thought of that. But what could I say?"

Marcy shrugged. "Tell him you're sick, going into the hospital. Something like that."

"Well, that very well may be what happens the way I'm feeling."

As it turned out, however, the ruse wasn't necessary. When she placed another call that night, expecting to hear the familiar recording, Greg himself answered her.

"Hello?" He sounded hoarse and exhausted, as if he had a bad cold. For a moment Renee struggled with what to say to make sure he didn't hang up on her.

"Greg, please, don't hang up. It's me. Renee."

There was silence on the other end, but there was no click.

"Are you there?" she asked, her heart pounding in her throat.

"Yes."

Renee swallowed. This was going to be difficult. More so than she had imagined. But hope swelled within her that he still hadn't hung up.

"Greg . . . I . . . we need to talk. There's so much you don't know. So much I need to explain."

Silence.

Renee swallowed again and plunged on ahead. "I know you think I deceived you, used you, which I did, I admit it fully. And I'm ashamed of myself. More than you'll ever know. I should have been straight with you from the first, but—but, well, I was just too stupid to see that I was being a fool." She was talking much too fast, but she couldn't help herself, she had to get it all out.

She took in a shallow breath and continued. "But if you'll let me tell you the whole thing . . . about Louis, well, maybe you'll understand better."

"What was he doing when I walked in?" He spoke so suddenly that Renee was taken off-guard.

"He . . . he had just gotten back from Europe the previous day and he'd come over to . . . I was breaking it off with him."

"I meant what was he doing to you. It was obvious I'd interrupted something."

Renee felt her face flushing in reference to that

sordid situation. If she ever saw Louis Mandol again, she would not be responsible for her actions. But she had to tell Greg what had happened. She couldn't discredit herself further by adding to her lies. "He was kissing me. Assaulting would be a more appropriate word. He wouldn't take no for an answer," she insisted. "You can't imagine how grateful I was when you walked in."

Greg snorted and Renee cringed at the sound of it. This was harder than she had imagined.

"Oh, Greg, I know how unbelievable this all sounds, but really, it's true. I—I'm no good telling you this over the telephone. We . . . I need to see you in person." She hesitated and then said in a small voice, "I hope that is possible. When will you be back in L.A.?"

"I have no idea." His flat, unemotional tone sent a flash of panic through Renee. She hadn't made an impression on him at all. Wildly she searched her brain for something, anything that would help her see him again—and soon.

"Then perhaps I could come up to Seattle to see you." She didn't wait for him to give his approval or disapproval, knowing she couldn't stand to hear a rejection, so she rushed right on. "In fact, I can take this Friday off as a sick day and fly up then."

When he still didn't answer, Renee took it as at least not an outright objection and she added, "I'll stay in a hotel somewhere near the airport. I can either take a taxi or the use the hotel limo service. Or I'll rent a car—whatever." She was talking too fast, almost frantically, but she couldn't help herself.

"I take it you're really serious about this?" Greg asked dryly.

"Yes," Renee said firmly. "I am. I deserve at least one chance, Greg, to explain my situation. And I hate talking over the phone about it." She hesitated and drew in a deep breath, letting it out slowly. "I'll see you on Friday, then, all right?"

"I don't know when I'll be home from the office," Greg said noncommittally.

"That's okay," Renee hastened to assure him. "I'll call you when I get in and if you don't answer, I'll leave a message on your recorder." She hoped that wasn't necessary. She hated the damned thing by now. "Okay?"

"Yeah."

"Well, see you on Friday," she said brightly.

"Whatever." Click.

Renee lowered the receiver and gulped painfully, weakness flooding through her until she thought she might faint. It had hurt to the core, hearing Greg speak to her in that tone of voice. She was so used to the other Greg, the friendly, considerate, loving one. But at least she'd gotten through to him, at least she still had another chance.

Relief mingled now with anxiety as she pondered the possibility that he might choose to ignore her again, let her think he wasn't at home when she got there. Maybe not even be there at all. After all, he couldn't have sounded less enthusiastic about her coming. But still, she couldn't see him being that cold-hearted, knowing she was going to a lot of trouble to fly up and see him. Which reminded her, she ought to get on the phone and make reservations—

airline and hotel. It would seem strange, staying in a hotel when Greg had a perfectly adequate apartment, especially when they'd spent so much time together alone at her place. But things were different now, she reflected bitterly. God help her, but she hoped it wasn't too late to change them back.

She barely slept Wednesday night and on Thursday hardly ate a thing all day long. But by Friday morning an exhausted calm took over and as she sat beside Marcy, who had offered to drive her to the airport before she went to her office, Renee could hardly believe she felt so relaxed. The calm before the storm, she mused wryly.

"Well, kiddo, here we are," Marcy said as she pulled into a vacant spot in the departure lane of the Western Airlines terminal.

"Thanks for the ride, Marcy," Renee said with a smile. "And the support."

"You're doing the right thing," Marcy assured her. "This guy is just too good to let slip through your fingers."

"He might have already slipped through," Renee said with a sobering expression.

"Now, don't start thinking like that. Think positive, act positive, and something positive is bound to come of it."

Renee smiled again and got out of the car, pulling her bag out of the back seat. "You're beginning to sound like a therapist, Lindstrom."

"Not anything that drastic. Just a realist."

"Well, guess I'll see you on Monday. Or late Sunday night if you're still up."

Marcy waved and put the car in drive but kept her foot on the brake. "Have a good time."

Renee looked doubtful but managed a cheerful face as she waved back.

She had made a reservation at a Holiday Inn near the airport in Seattle. As she rode in the hotel bus that she had called to pick her up, her gaze remained transfixed on the fog-shrouded landscape through the window. Her flight had arrived in mid-afternoon, but already the skies were darkening; low-hanging clouds promised rain, possibly a downpour. The heavy humidity had gripped Renee as soon as she'd stepped outside of the air-conditioned terminal.

Ah, well, a fitting atmosphere for what was surely the strangest trip she had ever made. She'd traveled alone before, of course, twice to attend management seminars, one in Dallas, the other in Atlanta, and on numerous occasions to see her parents who now lived in Florida. But this . . . this journey had an aura of unreality about it, as if she weren't really here, soon to be checking into a hotel alone, for the sole purpose of wooing a man she was on the verge of losing altogether, if not already.

A little sight-seeing on the way from the airport to the hotel would have been helpful in getting her mind on something else for a few minutes, but the thick blanket of fog obscured everything beyond fifty yards.

There wouldn't have been that much to see anyway, Renee discovered; the trip from the airport to the hotel was very short. After checking in and setting her one piece of luggage down on the floor,

Renee checked her watch and decided that it was probably a little too early to try reaching Greg. But, damn, she was getting nervous again. She drew back the curtain from the window, but even the prettily landscaped courtyard below did nothing to calm her anxious state. For one thing it too was drenched in the heavy, soggy atmosphere that seemed to be worsening by the minute.

Turning away from the window, she sighed heavily and then switched on the television set. The sounds of a familiar late-afternoon talk show were soothing, and she kicked off her shoes and settled back on the bed. By the time the first evening news program was over, in which the weather forecast predicted heavy showers at any moment, Renee decided it was time to call Greg.

Immediately after the first ring there was a click and the familiar recording. "Damn it!" Renee muttered, gathering herself sufficiently to deliver her message with a coolness and composure that had by now completely deserted her.

What if he didn't call her back? What if he had no intention of seeing her? She didn't think she could stand it, sitting all alone in this hotel room. Raindrops were beginning to patter against the windowpane, at first sporadically, then with an increasing steadiness, a dire warning of more than a mere summer shower. For a moment she felt as if she were going to cry.

Renee went into the bathroom and drew a tubful of steaming water, then pulled out her cosmetic bag from her suitcase. She could spend the time doting on herself, giving herself a manicure, washing her hair, maybe a facial. Anything to dispel this ever-increasing knot in the pit of her stomach.

Anything to erase the suspicion that perhaps this wasn't going to be a successful venture after all.

CHAPTER TEN

By eight o'clock she was almost beside herself. She'd called twice more and there was still no answer. By now anxiety and fear had escalated into anger; anger that perhaps he had lied to her just for revenge; letting her come all the way up and knowing he was not even going to be here after all. Or, worse yet, home all the while with the message machine on, but not willing to see her. But what could she do? She had no idea how to get to his apartment, and even if she asked someone for directions she wasn't so sure she wanted to risk getting out in what looked to be worsening weather conditions unless she knew exactly where she was going.

There was nothing to do but wait, maybe keep calling until he answered. If he did at all. The extensive beauty regimen she'd indulged in lost its usual power for setting her in an easier frame of mind with all the mental energy she was expending worrying over her plight. Whatever effect the facial had had on her complexion was marred by the taut gathering of worry lines on her brow.

By nine o'clock Renee was almost livid, cursing Greg for being such a spiteful, inconsiderate jerk and herself for being so gullible as to believe him when he'd said he'd be home tonight. For the sixth time she jerked up the receiver and dialed his number, not believing it was actually him answering instead of that infuriating recorded message.

"Hello?" he repeated.

Renee flinched at the sound of his voice—his real live voice! Making the utmost effort to control her exasperation she said, "Hi, it's me, Renee. Did you just get in?"

"As a matter of fact I just walked in the door." He didn't sound unfriendly, but neither did he sound particularly interested in hearing from her.

She knew she should refrain from asking, concentrate on not saying anything to get his ire up, but she couldn't resist at this point. "Did you . . . were you busy today?" *Why the hell weren't you home hours ago?*

"Yes. I was with a client until an hour ago." So cool, so unconcerned. Almost as an afterthought he added, "How was your flight up?"

"It was fine. I'm glad I arrived before all this bad weather started up though."

"Yeah," Greg said with a sigh. "I had to drive through it just now myself. The traffic's jammed up everywhere."

Lord, why did people have to insist on small talk,

herself included. She wasn't calling him to discuss the weather, that was for damn sure.

She cleared her throat and said, "Uh, Greg . . . listen, when would be a good time for me to come over?"

Silence. Renee's heart began tripping erratically. God, she had so much on the line here. Why couldn't he have a little heart and ease up on her just a little? He was making this every bit as hard for her as he possibly could. But she relaxed some when he finally answered. "I wouldn't advise getting out in this mess right now. Tomorrow would be better."

"Morning then?" She wasn't so anxious to drive now either, but she sure wasn't going to spend half the day hanging around here either.

"I guess so."

Renee's shoulders slumped in relief. Well, that was one hurdle cleared. "Okay. Can you give me directions to your place then?"

After telling him where she was staying, Renee jotted down the directions he gave her and then said good-bye. He obviously wasn't going to discuss anything further over the telephone and she really didn't care to either. Immensely relieved that she had finally gotten through to him, Renee undressed and switched on the television. She propped herself up in bed, and after staring at the meaningless pictures and sounds on the tube for a few minutes she drifted off to sleep.

The drive to Greg's apartment wasn't too difficult. It was some thirty minutes from the hotel, probably less if the traffic hadn't been quite so bad. But the rain continued this morning, slowing even the Saturday morning traffic to an occasional snail's pace.

Greg's address was in a rather swank, relatively newly constructed condominium-apartment complex. Of contemporary design, it was all sharp angles of wood and glass and brownish-red brick chimneys that seemed to extend from every unit. So very different from the ancient duplex she and Marcy rented. Renee wondered now what he'd thought of her place, though real estate values placed it at least as high as the most expensive unit in this complex.

She found the number of his apartment easily, but stood before it for a long, composing moment before pressing her finger to the doorbell. As she waited she began to tremble inwardly.

She was just about to chew on a fingernail—a childish habit she indulged in during times of stress —when she caught herself and held it firmly to her side.

Renee's heart did a little flip as the door drew back and he was suddenly standing there. Dressed in a pair of faded, worn jeans and burgundy knit pullover, both of which outlined and accentuated his lean, muscled body, he was the epitome of masculinity to Renee's way of thinking. It was all she could do to keep from throwing herself at him, begging him, pleading with him. But, no, she had to take this step by step. And from his expression he would be far from receptive to any sort of emotional scene.

"Hi," she said, forcing the tremor out of her voice. "Am I too early?"

Greg shook his head and opened the door wider, motioning for her to come in. "No. I'm on the telephone at the moment though." His lightly shadowed face—he obviously hadn't shaved yet—held not the slightest hint of interest in her presence and Renee felt a sinking sensation inside. *Forget about the way you feel,* she reminded herself firmly. *It's unimportant at this stage.*

"Oh, go ahead. I'm sorry I . . ." She closed her mouth slowly; he was already walking down a hallway away from her. "O-kay," she said beneath her breath, watching as he disappeared into another room.

Shutting the door behind her, she turned and walked across the small marble foyer and had a look around. It was a truly beautiful home; the kitchen, to her left, was a wonderful concoction of colorful Italian tiles and butcher block counters. She wondered how much time he spent in here; it struck her then how much of Greg Daniels remained a mystery to her.

At right angles to the kitchen was an oversized doorway leading to the living room. Renee stepped down onto the plush dark-brown carpeting and marveled at the design of the room. Rainy-gray morning light filtered through a skylight in the sixteen-foot ceiling, and to the left above was a catwalk lending access to an open-view display of wall-to-wall bookshelves. Contemporary furnishings in beige and ice-blue shades were scattered about the ample room and the walls were decorated with an odd, yet interesting assortment of Indian art and handsomely framed Cézanne prints. An interesting, personalized room, Renee mused appreciatively.

Greg's footsteps were soundless on the completely

carpeted floor and Renee jumped at the sound of his voice.

"Have a seat," he said quietly.

"Oh! Are you finished with your phone call?" What a stupid question, Renee chastised herself.

"Yes. But I'm afraid there will be plenty more this morning."

Renee sat down on a love seat, placing her purse down next to her. "Are you working today?"

Greg nodded and ran a hand through his thick hair. He looked tired, Renee noticed for the first time. And as he sat down on the couch opposite her, she could see that he really was. There were shadows beneath his eyes and she wondered if perhaps he was sick.

"So," he said, looking directly at her with those startling, grass-green eyes. "You came here to talk. So talk."

Renee shifted uncomfortably. He sure wasn't beating around the bush. She, however, could have used a bit more small talk this time. Nervously, she cleared her throat. "Yes. I do want to talk. I want us to talk. There was a misunderstanding and I'm truly sorry for what it caused."

"What's that?"

Renee looked at him in surprise. "Your walking away like you did."

Greg nodded. "Oh, you call *that* a misunderstanding."

"Yes," Renee said fervently. "It was. Believe me, Greg."

His expression was as skeptical as ever, however, and Renee went on. "As I already told you, yes,

Louis was trying to . . . Greg, he was practically mauling me. Until you got there. He didn't want to listen to me. I wanted him to go. I was breaking it off with him for good, and his fragile male ego couldn't take it."

Greg studied her thoughtfully for a moment, as if actually considering her statement. When finally he spoke, Renee cringed inwardly at the coldness of his tone. "Whatever you were or weren't doing with him is not the issue. You lied to me, and in doing so took advantage of me, my feelings, the feelings I thought were building between us, Renee. You made a fool out of me."

A sense of déjà vu washed over Renee as she recalled hearing those very same words, "took advantage of me," uttered by herself to Louis on so many occasions. And she had felt taken advantage of, made a fool of, so many times. All Louis had wanted was *her* time, *her* commitment, when he had given so little of either to her. All that had been very real, very understandable. And now Greg was saying the same thing. Somehow Renee just couldn't believe that the situation could reverse itself this way, that Greg was feeling as put upon as she had. But she'd better believe him, she'd better consider every damn thing he was saying with utmost seriousness.

Staring at her hands that lay primly folded on her lap, she said softly, "Greg, I didn't mean . . . Oh, damn, there's no point in lying about it now." She looked up at him. "Yes. I did lie to you. For all my own selfish reasons. I thought I would be getting back at Louis for doing the same thing to me." Agitatedly, she ran a hand through her hair. "God, it was so stupid of me. I didn't even want him anymore, though I didn't know that at the time. I want you, Greg. I . . . I love you." There, she'd said it at last.

Greg's snort jolted her like a vicious slap in the face. He got up suddenly and all she could do was stare with wounded eyes as he walked out of the room. Her chest pained her, as if someone were squeezing it and she had to stand up to ease the pressure. God, what else could she do? He obviously didn't believe her; not one thing she had said had made an impression on him. She could hear him moving around in the kitchen now. She stood stock still, unsure of what to do next. Should she leave, give up completely? He couldn't have made his disgust with her presence any clearer.

No! a resisting voice insisted. She loved him and she'd come a long way to prove it to him. She wasn't about to turn right around and head back at the first showdown. Bringing her arms up, she rubbed them and stared up through the skylight, watching the dreary, heavy clouds drifting past. No, she would stay and fight. She owed that much to herself and her future. The fact that Greg objected so strenuously to her deceit only made his character that much more admirable, increased her love for him all the more. It didn't matter what his reasons were for being so stubborn—a past love affair gone wrong or a wounded male ego—she didn't need to know any of that. All she needed to know was how to get him over it, to forgive her, and trust her enough so they could go on with what they'd had.

She thought of how she would have felt if the situation were reversed. Would she have been so willing to forgive and forget? Would not her pride have been equally offended that she had been used? What would it have taken for *him* to have gotten her back? No more than what she should be willing to give now to get Greg back. A tiny spark of hope flickered within her as she thought of what she must do and how to go about it. It might not work, but then again, it very well might.

She found him standing in front of the refrigerator, door open, frowning at the empty shelves within.

"You don't have very much in there," she commented, her tone indicating that she'd considered his rebuff inconsequential.

"No kidding," Greg said crossly, slamming the door shut and opening the one to the pantry. A brief glance revealed nothing more than a couple of boxes of crackers and an odd assortment of canned goods. It was close to noon by now and Renee herself was beginning to feel hungry.

"Did you eat breakfast?" she asked.

Greg shook his head and opened a box of crackers and withdrew a handful.

"Listen, I have an idea," Renee suggested eagerly. "Let's go out for something. I'm hungry too. We could brave this awful weather for something better than a box of crackers."

"You don't have to worry about me," Greg said, turning away from her to open a cupboard. Extracting a glass and opening the freezer for ice, he added, "If you're hungry, get yourself something to eat."

Renee's insides curled, but she resisted succumbing to the rejection. "I'm not really in the mood to eat all by myself."

Greg shrugged unconcernedly and Renee proposed, "I'd like to take you out."

Greg cast her a dry look. "You what?"

"I want to take you out," Renee repeated. "Wherever you'd like to go. Whatever you'd like to eat. Just name it, you got it."

His green gaze leveled on her for a moment, and then he turned to fill his glass with tap water. "Don't bother," he muttered.

"It isn't any bother," Renee insisted gaily. "You're hungry, I'm hungry, and you haven't got a thing in this house. Don't be so stubborn, Greg. Just get your jacket, or whatever you need, and let's get going."

Whether from the force of persuasion in her tone or his own physical needs, Greg finally relented and agreed to let Renee treat him to lunch. The ruse was only successful in appeasing their appetites, however, as Greg was no more communicative than before. As determined as Renee was to pull him out of his sour mood, he would not give an inch, obviously determined to sulk as long and as much as he wanted to.

They had taken Renee's rental car and as they drove into the parking lot of the complex, she purposely slowed down, pulling into the same slot she had used before. The steady drizzle, which was supposed to continue all day, suddenly increased, pounding down against the windowpanes in sheets.

"Wouldn't you know, it waits until we're ready to get out to start this up," Renee said with a grimace.

Greg, placing his hand on the door handle, said, "Just have to run for it then."

Impulsively, Renee leaned across the seat and slapped her hand over his. "No, wait!"

Greg looked at her with a surprised frown and Renee bit her lower lip as she held his foreboding gaze with her own. "I mean . . . it'll probably pass over in a minute. There's no use getting all wet if we don't have to." She smiled. "We should have brought an umbrella."

"Well, I would have if you hadn't been in such a hurry to leave," Greg said gruffly.

"I know," Renee said softly. "Sorry about that." She fiddled with the keys in the ignition for a moment, studying the way a certain section of hair curled on his nape as he turned his head to stare out the window.

Then, impulsively, she slid across the seat next to him, draping her arm around his shoulders. Greg looked at her in surprise. "What is it?" he asked, frowning crossly, not willing to give up one inch of his bad mood.

But Renee steadfastly held her cheery air. "What do you mean, what is it? Does a girl have to have a special reason to hug her favorite man?"

Greg rolled his eyes and turned his head once more, keeping his arms securely folded over his chest. But Renee was determined and she scooted up onto one knee to accommodate herself to his height. Placing her other arm around his other shoulder, she linked her hands together, trapping him within the circle of her arms. Undaunted by his posture—this was like embracing a rock—Renee lowered her head slowly, her lips hovering just above his ear. She felt him stiffen even more as her lips gently nibbled the flesh of his earlobe. She waited a moment, and when he made no objection, softly circled the rim of his ear with her tongue, breathing her hot moist breath into the labyrinthine contours.

Renee felt a deep shudder course through him at her touch, an electrical impulse that ignited a burning response within herself. Yet she was careful not to push too hard. She didn't want to scare him off completely.

Unlinking her hands, she brought one up to caress the side of his face turned toward the window. Still he would not turn his head, so she was forced to raise herself up a little more. She moved her lips carefully across the edge of his face, down the hard ridge of his jawline, then brushed them across the taut line of his mouth. Plying softly with her lips, she felt him respond again. With her other hand she turned his head even more toward her and ran her tongue along the outer contours of his mouth, then between his now moistened lips. Slowly, reluctantly, they became pliant enough for her to penetrate with her tongue. But again she waited, not wanting to rush too much, for her heart was pounding furiously by now and the last thing she wanted was to lose control with him, especially at this delicate point.

Ever so gently, and with utmost patience, she eased apart his lips, invading the inner warmth of his mouth with her tongue, exploring all the recesses and contours she remembered so well, had hungered for so much. Though Greg retained his passive posture, his resistance was weakening and her hand, which had slipped down to just above his folded arms, could feel his own increasing heart rate.

Applying pressure against one muscled arm, she managed to push it down out of the way, allowing her hand to rest against his breast. Spreading her hand flat, she felt the bud of his nipple against her palm. Slowly her hand began to massage the small erect bud into a rigid knot beneath her palm. Renee's breath caught in her throat, his instinctive response firing her own need, her passion to greater determination. Her hand left his stimulated breast, inching its way down the center of his chest, possessing the hard, flat plane of his belly. At the waistband of his jeans, she stopped, then dipped her forefinger downward for just a moment. Then, stoically ignoring the burning need within her, she forced herself to stop completely, removed her hand, and with one final wet caress of his lips with her own, pulled away.

Greg's eyes were closed, the former tenseness of his features revealing the obvious passion he, too, was struggling to control. Filling her lungs with a deep breath, Renee returned to her side of the car and said brightly, "Oh, look, the rain has finally slacked off." Extracting the keys from the ignition, she opened her door, not daring to look back at him. "Come on, let's run for it."

Then she was out of the car, dashing through the slick puddles on the asphalt, heading for the front door to Greg's condominium. She waited as he made his way to join her, astounded by the change in temperature the rain had brought. It was strange; after such a deluge one would have expected a cooling effect, certainly not this sweltering humidity that clung to the skin. As Greg opened the door and they stepped inside, both were assaulted by a wall of the stifling air.

Renee blew air through her teeth and waved a hand in front of her face. "What happened? It feels like a heat wave moved through while we were gone."

Greg wiped a film of perspiration from his brow and said, "It's that damned high ceiling in the living room. It doesn't allow for enough circulation. For all the modern appearance of this place, they left out the most basic insulation and ventilation requirements." Hands on his hips, his shook his head from side to side. "I'll have to turn on the air conditioner."

Renee was glad he suggested it. "Why don't you install a few ceiling fans? That would help the circulation a bit, wouldn't it?"

Greg was walking toward the kitchen and said over his shoulder, "I plan on getting some. Whenever I have the time, that is. For all the money I've spent on this place, I've really had little time to take care of it properly."

Renee followed him into the kitchen and sat down on a barstool as she watched him get a glass from the cupboard. "I don't know, I think you've taken care of it really well. It's furnished beautifully and—"

"What the hell . . ." Greg placed the glass on the counter as he stared at the floor near the refrigerator.

"What is it? What's the matter?" Getting up off the stool, Renee walked over to where he stood and she soon saw what he was exclaiming over. A wide puddle of water covered the Mexican-tiled floor in front of the refrigerator, obviously coming from beneath it. Greg just stood there looking down at it, obviously nonplussed as to the source of the water.

"You'd better check your freezer," Renee suggested, and when Greg opened the door to the side-by-side, the root of the problem became apparent. The freezer obviously wasn't working, and everything inside, which fortunately wasn't very much, was soggy and dripping. All the ice in the ice maker had melted and dripped onto the floor.

"Damn!" Greg muttered. "What the hell's wrong with this now?" His irritation was obvious as he added, "If it isn't one thing, it's another. And of all days—a Saturday. I'll never get anyone out here today." He sighed disgustedly and reached for a limp package of broccoli. "Guess I'd better get this stuff out of here."

"You don't have any idea what it could be?" Renee asked, vexed herself with this incident which had put him right back in the sour mood she had been struggling to dispel.

Greg cast her a dry glance and said sarcastically, "Do I look like a repairman to you?"

"I didn't mean . . ." Renee hesitated, then suddenly snapped her fingers and put her hand on Greg's arm. "Wait a second, Greg." He looked at her in obvious impatience. "Where's your breaker box?"

"What for?"

"You need to check the circuit breakers. It was lightning terribly while we were gone. It's possible one of the breakers was tripped. Maybe the one to the refrigerator."

Greg said nothing for a second, then put the soggy box of broccoli on the counter. Turning, he walked out of the kitchen and down the hallway. "It's in here."

Renee followed him down the hallway to another smaller one branching off it. An inconspicuous metal door was at one end and as Greg opened it Renee switched on the hall light. Greg was staring at the multitude of switches as if trying to interpret an abstract painting. "Dammit, would you look at this," he said, gesturing with one hand. "Not one of the damn things is marked." He wiped his damp brow with his shirt-sleeve.

"That's okay." Renee stepped in. "You go on back to the kitchen and tell me if it comes back on."

Greg sighed heavily, then said, "Whatever . . ." He walked back down the hallway to the kitchen.

When he was there, Renee tried the first switch, snapping it all the way off then sharply back to the on position. "Was that it?" she called out.

"No," Greg shouted back at her, and Renee cringed at his deep angry tone. What a big baby he was!

"That one?" she called out as she flipped the next breaker.

"No!"

She continued with the next four breakers, continuing to get the same "No." Then, on the fifth, Greg yelled back at her, "All right. I think that was it."

Renee trotted down the hall to the kitchen and joined Greg at the freezer door. There was a recognizable hum of the motor accompanied by the softened whir of a fan. "Yeah! That was it, all right." She turned to smile at Greg. "You can put your broccoli back inside."

Hesitating first, as if he wasn't too eager to let her tell him what to do, Greg picked up the small package and deposited it into the freezer once again. "Well, thanks for the advice," he muttered reluctantly.

"Sure," Renee said brightly. "Anytime."

Greg drank two full glasses of tap water, then declared, "It's a damn oven in here. I'm going to turn on the air conditioner."

Renee helped herself to a glass of water, needing its cooling effects badly by now. She was just taking her first swallow as she heard a particularly vituperative expletive uttered from the opposite end of the hallway.

"God damn it! What the hell is going on around here?" Greg's voice growled menacingly and Renee put her glass on the shelf and hurried down the hallway to where he stood, hands on hips, jawline tense and rigid, his green eyes fixed on the small silver thermostat on the wall.

"What's the matter?" Renee asked cautiously. He looked ready to explode. The heat was already taking its toll on her nerves, too, although she dared not let them get out of hand.

"The god damn air-conditioning isn't working. I can't believe this. First the freezer, now this."

"It sounds like it's on," Renee said quietly.

Greg looked at her as if she had an I.Q. of 30. "Of course it's on. But it's just the fan." He held his hand up to a vent in a demonstrative manner. "It's blowing hot air."

Renee frowned contemplatively. "The compressor's not coming on then."

Sighing disgustedly, Greg said, "And of all days. This has got to be the hottest, most humid day of the year."

Renee had to agree with that. A steady drizzle was keeping up outside, but the effect on the already high temperature was like a steam bath or a jungle. Lifting her hair from the back of her neck, she thought for a minute, then said eagerly, "Greg, let's try the breaker box again. If that's what was wrong with the freezer, then it might be the same with the air conditioner."

Greg's expression eased a fraction and he nodded as Renee turned and made her way back to the breaker box. "Leave it on and let me know when you feel cold air coming out of the vent," she directed.

As she flipped through the various switches, ignoring the one for the kitchen appliances, Greg called out repeatedly, "Nothing."

Renee closed the switch-box door and walked back to join Greg, who by now was the epitome of absolute frustration. Renee tapped her forefinger against her lips. She was remembering something, a time she'd watched her father . . .

"Greg," she said suddenly, "where is your compressor unit?"

He looked at her with an even deeper scowl on his face. "Why do you want to know that?"

"The problem is obviously the compressor. The fan is working fine. Let me take a look at it."

Greg regarded her skeptically for a moment, then

said, "Next to the carport. Through the kitchen and utility room."

He led her through the kitchen and small utility room out the back door to the carport. An adjacent wooden enclosure with a gate housed the meter and compressor unit for Greg's condominium. Greg gestured with one hand and said, "You wanted to see it. Here it is."

Renee, by now totally irritated with Greg's persistent foul mood, chose to ignore it once again. "Good. I'll just have a look at it." Walking past Greg, she entered the small enclosure and began visually inspecting the rectangular metal structure. Bending over and stretching somewhat, she ran her hand across all of its surfaces, then glanced up at Greg. "Do you have a tool kit?"

Greg shook his head. "I've never needed one."

Refraining from the answer she wanted to give—you need one now, buddy—she said instead, lacing her tone with an appropriate amount of sweetness, "Well, would you happen to have a screwdriver, a Phillips? The kind with the pointed edge. Not the flat one."

Greg cocked an eyebrow. "I *know* what a Phillips screwdriver is. Yes, I have one." He turned and walked off to get it.

By the time Renee had unscrewed the bolts on the back of the removable panel and lifted the unwieldy piece of metal up and away from the unit, she was almost dripping with sweat. What an awful day, she thought, her energy sapped from just that small amount of activity. There seemed to be no movement of air whatsoever and what little of it there was felt heavy and oppressive.

But she was rewarded for her efforts by spotting almost immediately a tiny yellow reset button at the lower left corner of the exposed unit. She stretched awkwardly to reach it, but when she finally pushed on it, the compressor responded immediately, a blast of hot air gushing out across her leg.

"That was it!" she exclaimed delightedly, mindless now of the rivulets of perspiration dripping down her face. She scrambled up, to see Greg standing behind her, and caught the look of relief on his face. It was gone quickly, however, replaced by the uncooperative scowl he'd worn all day long. Nevertheless, Renee was encouraged by the first sign of relenting on his part. A damn small sign, admittedly, but a reason for hope.

The apartment was beginning to cool even as they shut the back door and walked into the kitchen. "It feels better already," Renee said cheerfully as she stood with her face tilted up to one of the vents, relishing the effect of the cooling air on her moist skin.

Greg was busy getting the glass of ice water he'd wanted earlier, and as he took a long swallow, he uttered a half-groan. "Thank God," he said, placing the empty glass on the counter.

Renee glanced at him disappointedly. After all the trouble she'd gone to, he could at least have the decency to acknowledge what she'd done. In a teasing tone she said, "Nice to have a woman around the house, isn't it?"

Greg's narrowed gaze held hers for a moment,

then he lifted a shoulder and gave a barely perceptible nod. Renee would have to be satisfied with that little bit of approval, for he said then, "Well, I've got some work to do." He started to walk away, then added in what sounded like an afterthought, "Are you staying?"

Renee's facial muscles tensed ominously for a dangerous moment before she got hold of herself and refrained from the rather acrimonious retort she longed to hurl at him. Oh, but he was being pigheaded! Somehow, though, the more stubborn he was about being so unforgiving, the more determined she was to see him give in.

In a tone that was becoming increasingly hard to muster, she said lightly, "Of course. You go on ahead and get your work done. I thought I'd go shopping and get something to cook for supper. You have a really nice grill on the patio. Would you care for steaks this evening? I grill a mean filet."

Greg shrugged and said in that infuriating noncommittal tone, "Suit yourself." Then he walked off down the hall toward his study.

Renee glared at his retreating back and gritted her teeth. Leaning back against the counter, she folded her arms across her chest and chewed on the inside of one cheek. *All right, all right, you heard what you just said, Renee, so go on and do it. The day—and the night—are far from over yet.*

She spent a long time in the giant supermarket that could almost be termed a department store. Greg's cupboards and refrigerator had looked so abysmally bare that she ended up buying quite a few staple items as well as the makings for the dinner she planned to cook for them.

Greg was still holed away in his study when she made it back to the condominium, so Renee set about emptying the large grocery bags and unwrapping the steaks. She searched the cupboard for an appropriately sized dish in which to marinate the steaks, washed the potatoes, and placed them inside the microwave, then went out onto the patio to turn on the gas grill.

How incredibly simple everything was nowadays, Renee thought. Wistfully, she remembered the camping trips she used to go on with her family, how they would cook on the old, dependable Coleman stove, nestle their foil-wrapped potatoes atop the barely glowing coals of the fire. No matter how one pre-seasoned, marinated, or tenderized, food cooked with all the modern conveniences simply didn't taste the same. Not, at least, to Renee.

She adjusted the fire to preheat the grill for the steaks, then went back inside the kitchen. She set about slicing lettuce and tomatoes and artichokes and mushrooms for the salad, then, putting them aside, found silverware and wineglasses with which to set the table. She'd even bought a couple of decorative candles. If you're going to do it you might as well do it right, she'd reasoned.

By the time she put the steaks on the grill she decided it was time to let Greg know dinner would be ready soon. She walked slowly down the hall and placed her fisted hand above the door for a second before knocking. Suddenly she felt intimidated; she wasn't so eager to see that tiresome scowl on his face, a visual upbrading for her intrusion on his privacy. Nevertheless her fist met the door and she tapped lightly three times. All she heard was an indistinguishable grunt, or groan, she couldn't discern which.

"Time for dinner, Greg." Still he said nothing, so she stuck her head in the door. She was completely surprised by what she saw. This was certainly nothing like the scene she'd imagined; Greg huddled over a batch of paperwork in total absorption, perhaps scratching a pen against the side of his head in thoughtful consideration of whatever it was he was working on.

There was indeed a stack of papers on the large walnut desk. But all of it, for the moment, was completely ignored. Greg lay stretched out on his back on the studio couch, one arm thrown over his face, one leg straight, the other bent at an awkward angle.

Renee frowned as she stepped into the room, feeling a mixture of irritation and concern over what she saw. All that time she'd been slaving away, shopping, cooking, and all of it for him, he'd been in here sleeping. Or at least part of the time he'd been that way. But maybe something was wrong—maybe he was sick or something.

Tentatively Renee approached the bed and stood looking down at him for a few seconds. "Greg?" she spoke softly. "Are you all right?"

After a long moment he gave a barely perceptible nod of his head. Renee said then, "Dinner's ready. Aren't you hungry?"

He shook his head slowly from side to side and

Renee's frown deepened in vexation. "Well, I sure do hope you get hungry soon. I went to a lot of trouble."

With a groan Greg turned onto his side and said in a sleepy voice, "Wake me in about ten minutes."

Renee placed her hands on her hips; at the moment that was the safest place for them. She would have liked very much at the moment to punch Greg a few times, good and hard. It occurred to her then that if this was what he was like, such an unbelievably stubborn mule-headed man, then perhaps she was hitching her wagon to the wrong star. But the doubt was little more than a fleeting thought brought on by her own irritation over the whole situation. After all, this whole mess was her fault in the first place.

So she left the room as quietly as she had entered it, then busied herself reheating the loaf of French bread and uncorking the wine. After ten minutes was up she marched back down the hall, knocked once, and entered the study.

"All right, Greg, ten minutes is up. If we don't eat soon, the steaks are going to dry out."

Whether from hunger or a sense of obligation, Renee had no idea, but after splashing some cold water on his face, Greg joined her in the dining room. She had gone to a lot of trouble in setting the table prettily, lighting the two dripless ivory candles, but if Greg was impressed by her efforts, he certainly didn't show it. Indeed, if he enjoyed her carefully prepared meal, he didn't let on to that either; he simply ate everything on his plate and drank each glassful of wine Renee poured him. As determined as she was to get some sort of response out of him, he was equally determined not to offer anything other than monosyllabic responses. By the time they were finished and Renee was clearing the table, she was beyond disappointment. She almost felt relief that it was over. So much for that tactic, she mused, running the dishes under the faucet before placing them in the dishwasher.

By now all the effort and energy she had expended throughout the day was taking its toll and all she was really in the mood for was to lie down and take a nap herself. But she couldn't. Not yet. She wasn't about to throw in the towel based on what little she had accomplished thus far.

Greg had gone back to his study, apparently to catch up on what he should have been doing all afternoon. Renee finished with the dishes, dried her hands, and looked around for something else to do. But she'd done everything that could be done here; the cupboards and refrigerator were full, the dishes all put away, the counters gleaming. With a forlorn sigh she wandered back out into the hallway, waited for a moment to hear anything coming from Greg's study, which she didn't, then stepped down into the living room. Her gaze swept it slowly, then settled on the stereo in one corner. She walked over to it and after a few minutes of figuring out the various dials, turned it on, adjusting the volume to a low level so as not to disturb Greg. She looked around for a magazine, anything to read, then lifted her gaze upward to the catwalk above. She climbed the narrow stairway to the platform that ran alongside the wall-length span of bookshelves and stood with hands on her hips as she quickly surveyed the wealth of books.

Then, moving closer, she began to read the titles, one by one, selecting one now and then that she particularly wanted to look at further. Reading was a favorite pastime for Renee, a particularly fortunate circumstance in this instance, as it appeared Greg was going to be holed up in his study for a long while.

She was curled up on the couch with a novel when Greg finally did come out to join her a couple of hours later. She caught his gaze as he stood for a moment in the doorway, her prone form hidden from his line of vision by the back of the couch; she was gratified by the expression he wore. Obviously puzzled as to where she was, she noted a glimmer of worry too. But as she rose up on her elbows and he saw her, he quickly schooled his expression back to its former stoniness. Renee wished for the hundredth time he'd just give up on this stubborn game he was punishing her with, but realized that it was totally up to him as to when he would ease up. If ever, she reflected soberly.

"Hi!" She greeted him with a warm smile, receiving none of the same in return, as expected. "Are you finished working yet?"

"Yeah," Greg said shortly. "Is there any more of that wine we had for supper?"

Renee sat up and lay the book down beside her. "No, we finished it all. But there's beer in the refrigerator."

Greg raised an eyebrow in apparent surprise, then turned and walked into the kitchen. Renee followed him and stood with her shoulder against the doorframe, arms over her chest as she asked, "Are you hungry? I can make some popcorn."

Snapping the tab off the can of beer, Greg said dryly, "I don't have any popcorn."

Renee smiled brightly and strolled toward the pantry, then opened the door. She held out a large bag of it for his inspection. "You do now." At Greg's wry glance she said, "I think of everything."

Greg gave an uninterested shrug, then took a healthy swig of his beer. "Actually, I'm not hungry."

"Neither am I," Renee conceded, placing the bag of popcorn back on the shelf. "Hey, let's watch television. I checked the schedule, and there are a bunch of good movies on cable."

"Like what?"

"Well, there's a Woody Allen, a Charles Bronson, an Italian—it's probably dubbed but—"

"I don't care," Greg interrupted. "Put on whatever you want."

She chose the Italian. The dubbing was awful but the mood was terrifically romantic. She had settled down in one corner of the couch, Greg on the love seat. After a few surreptitious glances his way, Renee could see that he was watching the movie too. That was good even if he wasn't paying any attention to her. Well, something could be done about *that,* she decided.

Two-thirds of the way through the movie she decided the time was right to make her move. Quietly she got up off the couch and just as quietly joined Greg on the love seat, careful to leave a respectable distance between them. Greg looked at her curiously for a moment, then turned his attention back to the movie. Renee was watching too, but her mind had ceased to register any of the plot or dialogue. When the last scene began to fade out, accompanied by soft strains of a bittersweet melody, Renee raised her hands over her head and stretched languidly.

"Mmmm, that was really good." She turned to face Greg, imperceptibly moving her body a fraction closer to his. "Did you like it?"

Greg shrugged noncomittally. "It was all right, I guess."

"Come on," Renee prodded playfully, shifting again and in the process positioning her body so near to his that their legs were touching. "You were captivated the whole way through. There must have been *something* you really liked about it."

"I like Mastrioanni. He's a good actor."

"Mmm, he is." Casually, as though unaware of her own movements, she lay her hand on his knee, and went on airily. "I don't know though. I thought Marianna was miscast. I would have thought someone, I don't know, a little older perhaps, would have fit the role of the mother better. She seemed a little young to have all those complicated emotions, don't you think?"

Again Greg shrugged, making Renee want to slap her palms down on top of each rugged shoulder and hold them still. "In my opinion the actors were well chosen," he said.

Previews of another cable movie were being shown and Greg focused his attention on the screen. Renee stared at his stubborn profile for a moment, then, deciding her store of small talk was just about exhausted, reached for the remote control device that lay on the chrome and glass coffee table and punched the off button. Greg turned to her suddenly, obviously surprised and irritated with her for doing so.

"What are you doing?"

"You don't want to watch any more of that, do you?" Renee's tone was sweetly coaxing and the fingers of one hand, which had sneaked its way to his nape, began to run lightly through his hair.

Greg made no reply, so Renee placed her cheek next to his, her lips grazing the angular line of his jaw, stopping to rest on his ear as she whispered seductively, "There are a lot better things to do than watch television, don't you think?"

Greg remained rigid, though Renee's other hand, which had moved down and across his chest, noted the increase in his heart rate. He wasn't as unaffected as he pretended, she thought with increasing confidence. Gingerly she placed her lips on his, sliding her tongue around the perimeter of his firm, resisting mouth. With infinite patience she nibbled the warm flesh of his lips, her hand on his chest moving in slow, tantalizing circles. When at last he relented the slightest, she plied his lips apart with her own, invading his mouth with her tongue. She could feel his initial response quickly, followed by resistance, but she was determined now. Placing both hands on his shoulders, she pushed him backward, tilting his head to a more accessible angle.

Then she kissed him completely, with an ardor and need that came from the depths of her being. It was a plea, a begging for forgiveness, a request to continue what they had once shared, and which she had foolishly almost thrown away. Never before had Renee opened herself up so completely; she was willing to give whatever was needed to mend the damage she had inflicted in the relationship. Surely he could find it in his heart to listen to her, to believe her, to forgive her.

And when, after responding with a fervor matching her own, he brought his hands up to her shoulders and pushed her backward, away from him, Renee simply stared at him in bewilderment. Surely he wasn't looking at her with that same blank, stoic expression, as if they hadn't even touched. But he *was* looking at her that way, and she gulped spasmodically when he spoke. "I'm going to bed now," he said. "If you watch any more television, be sure and keep it down low."

He could just as well have slapped her face. Somehow she found her voice, feeble as it was. "Wh-why are you going to bed, Greg? What's wrong?" she added shakily.

He slanted a glance her way for the merest second, then got up, casually running a hand through his hair. "Nothing's wrong. I've just got a headache. Good night."

Renee sat dumbly, too stunned to move. She stared at his retreating figure as he left the room, unable to believe that he had done it again—rejected her so coldheartedly, with such finality. It was simply too much to bear or believe.

CHAPTER ELEVEN

Exactly how long Renee sat in the same position, unmoving, unseeing, she hadn't the least idea. The one lamp that had been on earlier was still burning, the occasional swish of automobile tires on some distant damp street the only sound intruding on the quiet of the early morning. But Renee was conscious of only one particular sound echoing over and over in her brain—a door being firmly closed down the hall.

Greg's door. That one last message had seared her deeply, unforgettably. It was painfully clear now that what she had considered mere stubbornness was outright final rejection. There was no understanding, no vestige of understanding, no vestige of empathy that would have enabled him to at least give her a fair chance. She knew that now. But how grossly unfair, how cruel of him to have let her come all the way here when he'd known all along he wasn't going to forgive her.

Renee's chest ached with a pain that held her cemented to the couch. She just couldn't move. She hurt. Her heart hurt, her brain hurt, her pride hurt. But the unfairness of it hurt even worse. God knows she had done wrong, had lied to him, had taken advantage of him but she was sorry! How many times had she said it? He just didn't believe her, or was it just that her sorrow didn't make any difference? He just didn't want her anymore, and what else was there that she could do to persuade him otherwise? Nothing.

Physical reality gradually penetrated the stupor of shock. Her body ached from the rigid position it had assumed these past hours. Her gaze slowly wandered the room, taking it all in one last time. Then, with a deep, ragged breath, she placed her hands on either side of her legs and pushed herself up.

She stood, acutely aware of a bone-deep weariness. She rubbed her fingers against the inside corners of her eyes and pressed the palms of her hands against her face. The lump in the back of her throat threatened to expand uncontrollably; the corners of her mouth twitched wildly. She just wanted to cry, cry like a baby.

Where is my purse, she thought distractedly, glancing around the room. *Where did I leave it? Oh, yes, the kitchen.* Her suitcase, which she had planned on bringing inside earlier, was still in the car.

Her leather shoulder bag lay where she had left it, on the counter beneath the wall telephone. She was reaching out for it when suddenly she stopped, her gaze arrested by the small pad and pencil that lay next to it. She pressed the fingers of one hand to her mouth and contemplated it. Should she? But what else was there to say? Wouldn't her absence be explanation enough? He expected, wanted her to leave. Nevertheless, the impulse to have some sort of last say was stronger, and she reached out, pulling the pad and pencil toward her. Picking it up, she walked into the dining room and pulled out a chair. The light from the living room was dim, but just enough to see what she was doing.

Tentatively she picked up the pencil, poised it over the paper for a moment, then lifted the tip of it to her lips. She chewed absently on the end of it, staring upward through the skylight at the few stars now peeking out of the scattered clouds. She should write down all the things she had thought about these past few hours, all the reasons why she was right and he was wrong for not giving her a chance, expressing her anger over his refusal to see her side of the story. But her mind was too full of the pain of rejection, the sadness that she was leaving a man with whom she'd never expected to fall in love, but had, irrevocably so. The pity of it was almost too much to bear.

The carpet would have muffled the sound of his footsteps anyway, but as Renee was to reflect later, her painful reverie was really what kept her from hearing him come up behind her.

"Renee?"

She jumped at the sound of his voice. One hand on her throat, she jerked around to see him standing there, dressed in a pair of faded jeans. The sight of his bare, muscular torso was startling, riveting; she felt hot and cold simultaneously.

"What are you doing?" Greg asked. He glanced pointedly at the pencil she was still holding.

"I . . ." She cleared her throat and looked down at the piece of paper she had begun writing on. *Dear Greg* was as far as she had gotten. "I was writing you a note," she answered feebly.

"What for?"

Renee looked up at him and was puzzled by the strange expression in his eyes. "I—I don't know really."

Impulsively she snatched up the single sheet and crumpled it in her palm. "It was silly. Wasn't important." She swiveled around and suddenly he seized her wrist, making her turn back to him.

"Tell me," he insisted in a low tone. "Tell me what you were going to write."

Renee's gaze wavered for a moment beneath his demanding eyes, then gradually steadied as she became aware of what was really happening. He obviously wanted an answer to his question, and why shouldn't she give him one? It was what she wanted, wasn't it—the last word?

"All right. I was going to tell you good-bye, since you didn't give me the chance earlier. I was going to tell you how sorry I am. Sorry for deceiving you, for using you, which was wrong, very wrong." Her voice dropped. "Sorry that it's over between us." She blinked once, looked down, then lifted her gaze to his again, this time directly, uncompromisingly. "And sorry, very sorry for you—that you have to be so rigid, so unbending, so unwilling to even give me a chance. I did nothing really, Greg, except lie to you. And that wouldn't have been possible if I hadn't been lying to myself also. Believe me, I'm the one who came out with the short end of the stick. You've been deceived, but I've lost everything. I—I . . ." Her voice faltered and suddenly her throat felt clogged up, her vision blurred and her chest felt as if it would cave in. She chewed her upper lip then brought her free hand to her mouth. Her gaze dropped and she wished desperately that she were in another room, anywhere that she didn't have to hold back this emotion that threatened to erupt.

Greg's silence was almost more than she could endure. What else did he want from her? That she should make a complete fool of herself, break down and fall at his feet? Suddenly Renee knew that she wasn't beneath doing such a thing. At least he was still standing here; why shouldn't she give one last go at it? What more could she lose?

Still looking at the floor, she drew in a deep breath and let it out slowly. When she spoke her voice was surprisingly calm and direct. "Greg, whatever happens—whatever you end up deciding about us—because it's totally *your* decision, you know, I . . ." she swallowed then continued, "I really love you. I'll *always* love you. God knows I never intended to, but dammit that's what happened. I don't think I thought you were for real in the beginning. I didn't know a man could be so . . . so wonderful." She gave a small sardonic laugh. "I guess I was too used to thinking I was in love with Louis." She winced. "I still can't believe I was so naive. I thought *he* was a real man, the perfect specimen. By the time I met you, Greg, I was at the point of just about going crazy dealing with that self-centered egotist. All I wanted to do was get back at him." One corner of her mouth twitched as she added softly, "I certainly never intended it to lead to this."

She was looking back down at the floor again and when Greg suddenly reached out and took both her hands, tugging her until she stood, she looked up at him in wonder and confusion. Placing his hands on her shoulders he drew her toward him. "Come here," he whispered, pulling her to him. The move was more than she could bear. Suddenly the dam within her shattered and tears were coursing down her cheeks in small rivers. Placing his hand on the back of her head, he muttered, "Shhh," over and over but Renee was beyond being shushed now. She was crying, blubbering against his chest like a little girl. She couldn't stop herself so he let her go on for a few minutes until the storm subsided.

She sniffed, her breathing noisy and ragged. Shed of the emotions which had gripped her blindingly, she became acutely aware of exactly where she was. Greg's chest was damp against her cheek and the small crisp hairs tickled her nose. But what was he doing, holding her like this, stroking her neck and back, murmuring something unintelligible in her ear?

She pulled back and looked up at him with red, swollen eyes, frowning in bewilderment. In answer to her unspoken question, Greg said quietly, "Come on, let's go in the living room." He released his embrace and, taking her by the hand, led her to the love seat they had shared earlier that evening.

He pulled her down beside him and suddenly she began to feel a revival of hope. But even that made her want to cry. Her mouth quivered ominously and Greg reached up to smooth her lips.

"No more of that," he said, gently lifting the corners of her mouth into a grin. It didn't hold, however, when he removed his hand, for Renee was too anxious to hear what he wanted to say.

"Now, first of all," he said firmly, "I want to refute what you said about my rigidity. In fact, I've always prided myself on being quite the opposite."

"But you—"

"Hush. Let me talk. I know I've probably been an ass, but . . . well, it was quite a shock when I walked in on you that day with what's-his-name."

Renee was about to insert Louis's name, then stopped herself. What's-his-name would do fine.

"Anyway," Greg went on, "I've seen nothing but red ever since then. I put a lot of value—a hell of a lot—in trust, and when I saw you there with him all over you I . . . I . . ."

"Greg, I've told you, I was trying to get rid of him. He made me sick—he was mauling me! You don't know how grateful I was that you walked in."

Greg shook his head. "All right. Enough of this. We've gone all over it and I believe you."

Renee's eyes widened and she said softly, persuasively, "Oh, Greg, I promise you. You can believe me from now until forever. About everything. I was just so confused then, so . . ." Something hit her then and she smiled up at him, shaking her head from side to side.

"What is it?" Greg asked, puzzled. "What are you laughing at?"

"Oh, I'm not really laughing. I . . . I just can't believe how wrong I was about you. Boy did I ever pick the wrong fella to use for revenge."

Greg said nothing but the sly expression on his face whetted her curiosity. "What? What are you looking like that for?"

He reached up to slide a forefinger back and forth against his upper lip, barely able to suppress a smile. "I got a little revenge of my own, you know—especially last night."

Renee's eyelids narrowed and she sat straight up. "What! Are you telling me you've been faking all this anger and irritation with my presence this entire weekend? Greg Daniels, you low-down, sneaky . . ."

"Hey, hey, don't get so excited," Greg interrupted. He ran his tongue inside one cheek for a moment, a contemplative expression on his handsome features. "I wasn't *entirely* faking, but I must admit it was nice to give you a little of your own medicine."

Renee's jaws tightened as she glowered back at him. "You turkey."

"You deserved it, Michaelson, and you know it. That little car scene was your dirtiest trick of all. What did you think you were doing? One more minute and that carefully controlled seduction would have backfired on you, babe."

Watching the seriousness of Greg's expression, something within Renee began bubbling to the surface and she suddenly reached out and poked him in the ribs with her finger as she smiled. "You know something Greg, if you think about it, this whole thing's almost ridiculous."

But Greg didn't appear too amused and Renee inserted hastily, "Greg, really, I just meant . . ." Her expression became serious once more and she stared at his chest for a moment, before raising her eyes to his, her voice whisper-soft as she spoke. "I just didn't count on falling in love with you after . . . after . . ." She hesitated, then gulped. How could she adequately term the physical union they'd shared, a passion that didn't relate to any other standards? "After the loving," she finished quietly.

And finally, wondrously, a slow, satisfied grin spread across Greg's handsome mouth as he pulled her to him, laying her head against his shoulder. "Well, I'm glad you did. You know, I kind of like that description."

"What?"

"After the loving."

Renee looked up at him and smiled, her eyes lighting up with pure happiness. "Me too."

There was a familiar sparkle in Greg's eyes as he said, "So . . . how about proving that you *really* mean it?"

And she did. Right then and there.

LOOK FOR NEXT MONTH'S
CANDLELIGHT ECSTASY ROMANCES ®

210 LOVERS' KNOT, *Hayton Monteith*
211 TENDER JOURNEY, *Margaret Dobson*
212 ALL OUR TOMORROWS, *Lori Herter*
213 LOVER IN DISGUISE, *Gwen Fairfay*
214 TENDER DECEPTION, *Heather Graham*
215 MIDNIGHT MAGIC, *Barbara Andrews*
216 WINDS OF HEAVEN, *Karen Whittenburg*
217 ALL OR NOTHING, *Lori Copeland*